GENTLEMEN, I ADDRESS YOU PRIVATELY

GENTLEMEN,
I ADDRESS YOU PRIVATELY

KAY BOYLE

CAPRA PRESS
SANTA BARBARA

(Earlier version published in 1933 by
Harrison Smith and Robert Haas, New York.)

Cover design by Cyndi Burt.
Typesetting by Stanton, Minneapolis.

LIBRARY OF CONGRESS CATALOGING-IN-PUBLICATION DATA

Boyle, Kay, 1902–
    Gentlemen, I address you privately / by Kay Boyle.
    p.   cm.
    ISBN 0–88496–318–7 : $18.95
    I. Title.
PS3503.09357G43   1991
813'.52—dc20   90–19863
                                                          CIP

CAPRA PRESS
Post Office Box 2068, Santa Barbara, CA 93120

"Gentlemen, I address you privately

and no woman is within hearing."

ERNEST WALSH

CHAPTER I

MUNDAY lay still on the bed, harking to the storm's cold anger, its stern ecclesiastical wrath speaking out in fury against man. It seemed that the sea had borne long enough with the great slab of winter cast down upon it, and now it had taken matters to itself, but in spite of the wind blowing there was a deep silence on the air, as if great banks of water stood still outside the house. The rain was falling black and wild on the skylight, and now it would not be long before living things, caught in the rearing tide, would come hastening over, dead, but writhing as if with life in the current. Now the tidal wave itself must have risen, Mundy thought, and he lay on the bed, harking to its presence. Depths of water must be standing solid in the streets below.

It was a bitter place he had come to, but the continent and the shape of it were clear in his mind. Up here in the north were the long unbroken sweeps of iron weather that melted downward through Paris, Dijon, Marseilles, until they were running molten on the southern coast. The wind of these parts wore itself thin in the north, in Dieppe, or in Le Havre even, with scarcely enough vigor left to cry out its heart in Brittany; but in the end Munday knew he would get away. There was a grim elation in his blood because he was lusty and tall, with a thick mane of hair on his head, and health like a stallion's. He lifted his broad

7

hand and touched with rejoicing the locks that were growing where once the tonsure had been; for his escape was fresh, and the taste of it still sweet to him.

His escape was a wide wind blowing clear the way before him. The rose window of any church had always been wine enough for his veins and the kind of eyeglass he would go blind for. But all over this country, and England as well, he had seen youths scarce out of their knee-pants whipped into priests' skirts, seen them riding bicycles maybe, with their teeth hanging long as eaves from under their virgin, unshaven lips and the down still fair and soft on their faces. Just as he himself had bowed down his head to the tonsuring, backing into the Church as into a stable, backing, backing, a quivering, shy stallion into the presence of the Church, wooing its patience, coveting its beauty. Not the first, he thought, to mistake its attributes for food and drink, and not the last to.

His escape was many things to him: it was the miracle of the fishes and loaves, and the miracle of women. It was so new to him, he would never have enough of it. He lay still with it on the bed in this town where even the stones of the street were strangers to him, and touched the miracle of his own hair in wonder. He lay harking to the storm's fury, flung down upon the skylight's glass, and touched the thought of women in his shy, unbridled mind. Ah, women, how he liked the look of them. How he liked the look of the Virgin Mary, carved out of wood, having nothing in common with divinity. Even in this unfamiliar town, fair Mary stood in the church, for it was there his steps had taken him out of need as soon as he set foot on French soil. She had a small human face, painted high like a whore's, and her neck sprang up from her blue robe as if to keep itself pure, from defilement. The one woman he had yet given much thought to was this one with peace and humility in her regard.

How she had ever withstood the pomp and the ceremony, and the hypocrisy of centuries, would always be a mystery to him. She was the soft bush of May-flowers springing up like lace at the portal, and the granite and marble of the Church was no place for her. Out of the flesh and into the wood they had transported her, where music and poetry and the heart's conniving might have captured him for all eternity as well, taking the notes of any organ as gospel and the arch of any nave whatsoever as the lifting of the spirit. Mary was human, but the qualities the Trinity possessed, each one of them was too aloof to give away, except for a small portion of the truth, as a poet shares his vision, or as St. Martin his cloak, always the half of it instead of the entirety.

He knew he was not quick to come to things and that each conviction was like fresh soil in which he must germinate and spread. It was his patience that gave him a mystic sense of himself and, as if in a dream, he recognized the somnolent as well as the waking being. He knew his own power was akin to that of the Levites and gave him an untamed, virgin strength. This patient being moved groping, slowly, endlessly in quiescence, but he gave it little thought now, knowing that it was moving on into new places. But awake in him was a strong, willful curbing of himself that constantly challenged whatever freedom he had gained.

He lay still with his thoughts, harking to the storm blowing, when the door of his room flew open as though from the wind, and a stranger came hastening in. The wild night was pushing for dear life at the house and sending long, fresh blasts across the room from the straining windows. Munday lay quiet on the bed and watched the dripping man force the door closed against the storm. He was slight and short, and he wore a drenched, black oil-skin cape. He stood on the uncarpeted floor of the place and looked sharply around. When his eyes came to the bed, all motion stopped short as if even the blood had halted in his body.

"Oh!" he said. "You're Mr. Munday."

In any place he would have been remarked for his uncommonly attractive face and the quantity of sun and wind marked on it, as well as for the blue eyes, blank as midday, and the elegant blond hair curled tight as a woman's all over his head. Bicycle slippers were laced tightly on his feet, as neat as a lady's glove.

"My sister told me to have a look in here." said the little man, and a flavor of Cockney spiced his tongue. "Ayton's my name."

Munday swung his legs in his blue wool trousers over the side of the bed, and felt for his shoes.

"Oh, yes, she came in for a lesson two days ago," he said.

The little man stood looking about the room: at the black stove on its high, curved, iron legs, at the piano, and at the narrow bed with the blanket tossed aside.

"I say, could I take this off?" he asked. Out of his glamorous black skin, the little man looked shy and humbled in his dark seaman's shirt and breeches. He held his cape like a poor drowned thing in his fingers, and bore it, dripping, to a hook on the whistling door. "She won't be coming in for her lesson tomorrow," he said, speaking over his shoulder to Munday. "I've just got back from the equator and my sister wants to spend the first few days with me."

"It's bad weather to be out so late," said Munday.

"The time got away from me," the little man said. He stood holding his hands, one within the other, to ease their quaking from the cold. "Will I make a fire?" he asked.

"There's no wood," said Munday. "I've not been here a week yet."

"I can do without wood," the little man said. Munday watched him stoop and lay hold of the papers stacked under the stove; his hands were small and hairless, like the hands of a child, twisting the paper into long, flat spears.

He grinned up sideways at Munday. "How does my sister play the piano?" he asked, his eyes everywhere, seeking, prying, appraising. He gave a look, either shy or sly, at Munday and lined the stove's black heart with paper.

"Oh, as well as anyone," said Munday.

"Ah, now!" said Ayton. "Not as well as you! She's only been at it a year, and you're a great man!"

"Ah, such a great man!" said Munday, and he laughed.

He sat looking at the secretive, fair face and listening to the words of the little man. They were music to his ears that he liked to hear playing.

"As a matter of fact," said Ayton, "I couldn't quite bring myself to call on you. I kept walking up and down outside."

"My God, in this storm—" cried Munday.

"Oh, for hours," said the little man. "Picking up my courage." The game of homage and deference he was playing suited him very well. "Cheering me up with a drink or two to make me the bolder." Suddenly he swung about and looked into Munday's face. "It's what I wanted to ask you, too, that put me off," he said, speaking fast. "It's would you play something on the piano for me? That's what it is. Maybe I'll be sailing off in a day or two, and I wanted to hear you play a tune before."

His eyes fell, shy as a girl's, before Munday who had crossed the floor and sat down before the piano keys.

"Where will you be sailing to?" said Munday. "I wouldn't mind sailing south myself."

There seemed less of youth to the little man now than Munday had at first taken it to be. He stood out of the shadow, under the naked bulb, with lines of weather and wantonness striped across his cheeks.

"Oh, that, I don't know," he said. "I don't know what the orders may be."

Munday's fingers stroked the keys, and the little man stepped close to the piano. But for all his intention, he listened ill to the music. He watched Munday's face as he played, a face compassionate and gentle, and allied to things that were not familiar to him, to things that were somehow beyond him and therefore held him captive. But after a while he took a flask from a back pocket of his seaman's trousers and held it out shyly. Munday ran his fingers off to the end of the keyboard and Mozart's *Eine Kleine Gigue* fell silent.

"What's that?" he asked.

"It's whiskey," said the stranger, almost fearfully. The case was laid thick with an armor of parrot-feathers. "It's pretty, isn't it?" he said. "I got it in Panama." Munday crossed the room and took the glass and the cup off the chimney-piece and set them down. There was no talk of his having played, and Munday asked no question, but raised the cup to drink. The little man stood quiet, not touching the full glass but standing, halted by the stove. After a moment he said, "Look, there's something else too. I came here because I've got into trouble and I thought you might be the kind, for all I know, that would help me out."

He spoke quickly, with his eyes travelling fast over the worn boards of the floor.

"What kind of trouble?" asked Munday, and he set down the cup and listened.

"Ah, what's the use?" the stranger said. "It isn't as if I had a friend in this part of the country. If that was the case, I'd have a word or two I could speak out to him. There's plenty to do in every part of the world, and I could do with any place almost. If I had a friend who fell in with my ways, or I with his, then he and I might go off and chance our luck together." He did not lift his eyes, but cast hurried glances at Munday from under his lids. "I've done the harvest in Fifeshire," he said, and then he looked up, quick and ardent. "They say it's a wonderful sight to see in Sweden. I was two years for the harvesting in the Highlands, and both times I won the Maiden!" He spoke eagerly now, as if in thinking of his life he had suddenly seen how many were its facets and its triumphs. "The Maiden, you know, is the last handful of corn that's cut, and the man or the woman who cuts it is sure to be married within the year. But I don't pay heed to superstition." He began to laugh. "I've got the two Maidens hanging in my room right now, dressed up like they do them with ribbons. That's all the use I've got for them, or for any other."

"Oh, come now," said Munday. His own somnolent being harked to these words, but what the truth of them was he did not know. "We're not of the same way of thinking," he said. "It was the Virgin Mary who saved me for myself. I won't hear ill of any woman."

"Ah if I had a friend in this part of the country," said the little man, his blond curls shining like gold on his head. "Maybe then it wouldn't seem like such a cold place to me. It's the heart of these parts that's cold, it never thaws out to another human being." He looked up, despairing, and shook his childish hands helplessly, helplessly before the world's immunity. After a moment he thrust them out of sight, as if he wanted to be rid of them. "It's wrong—isn't it?—to come to a stranger for help," he asked, "but I couldn't turn to a woman. I know a few of them here, but it ruins a man to be with them. A man must stay to himself, away from them, if he wants to become anything at all."

Between them they had emptied the little flask, and the music Munday wanted to play was waltzing and ringing aloud in his head, but first he must have the truth from this little man, and he asked:

"What trouble are you in?"

"No matter what happens to women, they can always pick up the threads of what's left after, and go on. But something goes wild in a man," the little man said, not answering Munday's question. "God knows how many times I've cried over Santos-Dumont and the way he fell into the sea off Monaco and other places, or when his balloon used to leave him sitting in the top of a tree somewhere with all his importance taken from him. Do you think any woman would lie crying for the thing that sends men out, whatever it is, looking for peace alone?" The youth had entirely faded from his face, but his stubborn mouth kept on speaking. "Or that man Beebe," he said. "He goes down under water, in the name of science, maybe, but he's escaping from something else. He gives you water like another atmosphere, and better than air, if you'll have it. If you mate with a shark you're safer than spliced with a woman, Munday."

"I've plenty of time," said Munday.

He could feel the slow pace of the whiskey coursing in patience and forbearance through his body. Each thing in its own time he would come to, and now it was the time to halt the stranger's distress. He watched him walking back and forth in his drenched and supple bicycle shoes.

"Well, then," said the little man, and he stopped short before Munday. "Have you ever been an outcast?" he asked.

Munday leaned back on the chimney-piece, his fingers, strong and broad, holding fast to the lapels of his workman's jacket.

"Yes," he said simply. "I was put out. I had to leave England." The stranger took a step toward him, but Munday paid no heed, for this other thing was on his mind. He could never bring himself to believe that he had been sent away. "Or rather," he said, and he made an effort to appear strong and immune; for, after all, whatever had happened to him he had still managed to survive. "I had to leave Thirsk," he said.

"Why didn't you tell me this?" the little man murmured. "Why didn't you speak this way before?"

"It still seems impossible to me," said Munday, "but I had to leave the place. I was in the order then. There was always some talk about the books I read, and one day I stepped out of the vestry, and there was the canon absolutely off his head. 'What piece was that you were playing when the collection was being taken?' he asked me. 'Scriabin,' I told him. It was my own transcription of the *Poème de L'Extase*."

"Ah!" Ayton stood, listening attentively to these words. "Was it for that," he asked after a moment, speaking almost in disappointment, "for that you had to go away?" Munday turned, heedless of the question, and went across the room. "And what will you do now?" the little man was saying.

"I've never been a free man before," said Munday, and as he spoke the pride in his own power again swept through him. "In one season I'll do one thing," he said, "and at another, another."

"That would suit me very well for myself," said the stranger. "On shipboard or anywhere else you like, there're few free men left in the world. I'd like very well," he said, "to follow the right time of year from land to land."

They stood looking at each other across the bare, tasteless room. It might never have been the abiding place of any man, so flavorless it was in any light. Munday saw the little Englishman's clothes, as casual as his own, clean and dark, and cut to serve working purposes well. And one thing more they had between them, was the thought growing slowly in Munday's head: a feeling for the weather and fog, and the sea and land.

The little man had started over the boards now, with his hands thrust down in his pockets and his dark trousers, still wet from the rain, taking on the shape of his childish legs. The "oi" and the "ing" of his Cockney voice had a pleasant sound to Munday, but the light in his eye seemed singularly craven, a blemish in the young man's face. Munday put out his hand and laid it gently on the stranger's shoulder. "Well, then, how can I help you?" he asked, inviting him to speak even as the Church wooed men to revelation. But the priestly manner, which his blood but not his reason recalled, had set Ayton to shaking as if with the cold. "Are you ill?" Munday cried out.

"Yes," breathed the little man, "yes, that is it." He passed his hand over his face, and scarcely audibly repeated the words, "That is it," he said. "Yes, yes, I am ill. I've been a long time coming here." He said it twice over in his soft, urgent voice. "I've been a long time on the way," he said, "from other countries, other people. I didn't know where you'd be or what your face would be like, I only knew that the rest of them were like bloody hounds after me. I don't know what to do next," he said "I don't know what to do."

Munday put his arm under him and carried him, light as a child, to the bed and laid him down on it; there he lay curved and fallen, extinguished, no bone or body left. Munday, the emissary of God now, the priest serving and saving the lost, unlaced and took off Ayton's shoes, peeled the wet socks from his feet, and chafed the cold flesh with his hands. The feet were brown and tough, and limber as a cat's paw, and as immaculately clean. on the soles of them was tattooed a ship apiece in full sail. In a while, Ayton sat up on the bed and looked at Munday.

"I think I want to be sick. Whiskey makes me sick sometimes," he said.

"It's all right," said Munday. "I'll make you a cup of tea."

"I say," Ayton said. "I've behaved awfully."

"Lie down now," Munday said, his voice that of a father speaking to his son. As he set the saucepan of water on the hot iron of the stove, and it hissed at him like a serpent.

The little man was sitting on the side of the bed now, holding his white face tentatively, as if it were a strange object he cradled in his hands.

"I'm afraid I'll have to stay the night here," he murmured.

"Of course, you will," said Munday. He could not have the man going out sick into the streets, falling down as he might, lying bruised and beaten by the storm. It was an act, if not of God, then of nature, that had sent the little man here for him to succor. "Lie down on the bed then," he said again. "There's a mattress in the corner that I can put down for myself on the floor. The water will be boiling in another minute. When it does I'll take you your tea."

CHAPTER II

I T was the knock on the door that roused them the next
morning. For a moment Munday lay still, asking himself how it was that he had come to be lying this way under
a cover on the floor. He could see the tufts of dust under
the bed beside him, and then, like a word spoken, he saw
Ayton's open hand, hanging down from the bed. Its youth,
its immaturity, seemed moving now to Munday, as if it
were an object of beauty begun and left incomplete. When
the knock sounded again on the door, Ayton raised his
golden head from the pillow and looked down at Munday.

"Who's that?" he whispered. Munday got to his feet and
ran his fingers through his hair. He had slept in his long-
tailed shirt and his socks, and now he pulled his trousers
on, and buckled the worn leather of his belt. Languorous
and easy, he reached for his faded canvas shoes, surveyed
their cord soles for a moment, then stooped to put his feet
in them, and laced them fast. "Munday," said Ayton in a
whisper, "don't let them in until you know."

Whatever it was that lit his eye with fear, it was not the
sight of the woman that Munday let in. She stood just inside the threshold, looking sourly from one to the other;
a stout woman, no longer young, with a small face set
queer as a crumpled handkerchief above her unruly flesh.
She stood staring in resentment at them, her gaze nar-

rowed and the brim of her felt hat brim running dark with rain.

"Ah, come in, Miss Ayton!" Munday was saying. "It's eleven o'clock, Mr. Munday," said the woman in something like contempt. "And I decided to come for a music lesson after all." Ayton sat up on the bed and smiled brightly at her.

"Hello, Edith," he said.

"Hello," said Edith, speaking as if she did not like the taste of the word in her mouth.

"I'm glad you got my message," said Ayton. He put a pillow behind his head and sat back against the headboard.

"I got no message," said his sister. She took off her wet jacket, scorning Munday's aid, and laid it across a chair.

"But I sent you a telephone call!" cried Ayton. "The Alsatian girls promised me they would call you and tell you that Mr. Munday was sick and I was staying here."

"Ah, I imagined!" said his sister grimly. "I've come for my music lesson," she said to Munday. "I suppose you can't refuse me that?"

She looked at him with her smile so polite, so really pleasant, that he thought she could not really be angry at all. But there was her upper lip, arched like an eagle's, quivering venomously above her smile.

"I'm afraid you were anxious," said Munday, but he did not relent. He would not let them make him a party to their conflict. His life was for other things and places; in a little while they would take themselves up and go.

"Anxious?" snorted Edith. "Anxious about what? You don't imagine this is the first time my brother has gone off on a rip? She sat down abruptly on the piano-stool and gave a grunt of laughter.

"A rip?" asked Munday, and he, too, began to laugh.

"Ah, you've a lot to learn about my brother, Mr. Munday." she said. "But it's you who are a surprise to me. I've heard so much of you from people who have heard you play." She pushed her hat far back on her head, and sat helplessly there squinting up at Munday. "That's why my brother is where he is, Mr. Munday," she said. "When you think you have him, he slips from under." Then she swung about and savagely struck the piano keys. "I've been waiting six weeks in this black town for him," she said bitterly, "and the first night home, off he goes playing the fool." After that she held her peace for a moment. "This isn't at all what I came here to say," she said.

"Oh, well," said Ayton with an uneasy laugh, as he pulled the bedcovers up to his chin. "Now that you've begun, you might as well go on."

"Oh, might I?" asked his sister sarcastically. She turned her grievous face up to Munday's, as if seeking a glimmer of understanding there. "I came here for my lesson, Mr. Munday," she said, sitting helplessly, before the piano. Her fingers had dropped into her lap, lying there thick and flushed, with the tips pinched narrow from the cold. "It's nothing new. Three years ago I sailed to Singapore to meet him," she went on. "And he kept me waiting six months there. He had taken a fancy to Sarawak and the life of the natives," she said. I had the whole world looking for him, and he was off living with the head-hunters because he liked the quality of their skin, Mr. Munday. And another time." She spoke, slowly, without agitation, but the same venomous smile distorted her upper lip. "Another time he sent for me, he was in irons in Port Said for having insulted a superior officer. It took me two months to get him out, and once I had him out, what do you think he did, Mr. Munday? He shipped on another boat without a word to me, and for a long time I had no idea where he was."

Ayton in his shirt-tails abruptly swung his legs from the bed and set his feet down on the floor.

"But then what did I do?" he asked his sister, but she had had enough of him.

"I'll fetch my music from my case," she said, and she did not look at him as he dressed. "I thought you and Ayton might become good friends," she said to Munday as she took the pages from the shabby case. "He's very susceptible to art," she said. "He used to do watercolors, Mr. Munday. I thought you might make something of him as an artist, if you had the time."

She set up the sheets on the piano, upside down without noticing, and then she sat down on the stool again.

"Mr. Munday," she said. "Look at me, what a fool I am. Don't give a thought to Ayton. You can't do any good to him, and you yourself, you'll do something to be proud of with your music. Take my advice, Mr. Munday," she said. "He's for an old woman. I can bear with what a younger person never could."

"But you're not old!" cried Ayton, and he went to her side and put his arms around her. Munday watched him press the woman's face against his open shirt. Her eyes were wrung small, and tears ran from them and down her plump, sallow cheeks.

"Ah, I've never met anyone like him," she said, and she made no move. "If ever I had any ambitions of my own, I don't know where they've gone, Mr. Munday." She sat looking down at her hands lying in her lap. "During the war," she said, "he didn't believe in going to fight. He was a little baby then, as if just learning to walk by himself and do without his sister, and off we went, the two of us, to Ireland, to the bogs of the land where no English people had been before. And there we squatted in the bogs in one fashion or another until the war was over. We lived on the things we grew ourselves out of the damp soil and we made out. I don't know how we made out, but we did, with our hearts broken for Roger Casement and all the rest of them."

Ayton reached out and gently laid a piece of grey hair

back from her face. "And then what did we do, Edith?" he asked.

"Ah, yes" she said, "then we went to Capri where we had a vacation-time together. There he was with me in the sun and the flowers, but do you think it ever matters so much, Mr. Munday, after things have happened to take your faith away? Do you think I didn't go to bed every night thinking that by morning he would be gone?"

"We had a fortnight there together," Ayton said.

"Ah, yes, we had a fortnight there together," said his sister with bitterness. "Ah, yes, a fortnight. Yes, that's quite true."

"And then we went on to Spain together," Ayton said.

"We saw the finest bullfights there," said Ayton, looking at Munday now. "Have you ever seen a Spanish bull-fight?"

"Ah, but I didn't come here to say any of the things I'm saying," Edith interrupted sharply. "You get me here, and then you make me talk."

Her hat was wagging on the back of her head and she looked in bitterness at her brother.

"You might as well tell him what happened next," Ayton said.

"Well, we went gallivanting off to Panama then," she said. "Ayton was third-mate on the boat that time."

And then her voice came to an end and Ayton touched her shoulder.

"Well?" he said. "Well, tell him what happened then."

"Ah, I don't remember," she said with a shake of her head.

"You must tell him," said Ayton, his voice soft and stubborn. "You must tell him. I want him to know."

"Ah, well," said Edith, shaking off the touch of his hand. "Ayton lost his temper on the ship because the captain wouldn't let him spend half the day in his diving things under the sea. He had such a craze for going under, and of course the captain wanted him for duty now and then on the bridge, or wherever it was. And what did he do but one day go under without asking the captain's by-your-leave, and up he came with a string of pearls worth more than the ship and the captain put together. He didn't say a word at the time, but when we got to Panama, he bought a grand house there with the price of the pearls, and there we were going to settle down and live like a brother and sister should for the rest of our lives."

"You've never seen such pearls in your life!" said Ayton.

Edith wagged her head. "However it was," she said, "we hadn't been a week in our house when didn't they bring a summons for Ayton for having stolen the string of pearls! There was an actress crossing on the ship, and she said she had lost a string of pearls identical to the one Skippy had found under the water. Whether she was lying or not we could never tell. Maybe it was true she had lost them overboard, but she never found out they were gone until she unpacked her belongings. Anyhow, there it was, and it made a lot of trouble for us. We had to pay a fine and sell the house, and on account of the police, we had to get out of the country."

Ayton went over to the window and sat looking through the fine, falling rain to the ships locked close in the harbor. When he turned back to his sister and Munday, his eyes were wiped clear of any trouble or concern. It was the sight of the ships that had done this, Munday thought, for they must have in the past been the only door to freedom that stood open for him.

"Ah, women," Ayton murmured. "I've never had anything but calamity from them. The string of pearls is just one example." "Ah, get on with you!" Edith cried out. She stood up and jerked her drab hat lower on her forehead. "He's back from the Equator with a lifetime of longings in him, Mr. Munday," she said. "I'll have to pamper him for a while."

23

She blew her nose a blast in her handkerchief, and standing before the glass hanging on the wall she did her best to set her hat at a more becoming angle

"God help me," said Ayton, his hand mocking the sign of the cross, and then he said no more.

CHAPTER III

NEARBY on the slope a little white goat was nibbling at what sustenance she could find growing out of the hard ground. She was sneezing into the herbs and wagging her tufted chin, and now and again she turned her cold, green eye in her skull to observe the two men, the alien invaders, who sat on the other side of the cliff. Here a spring of winter-furze was blooming, starting up from the tough rock in dark green bouquets, with the lips of the yellow flowers standing out from the thorns and moving in the wind as though in speech among themselves. The sun was no more than a blur in the sky, and there was little left of the sight of Le Havre beyond the hills.

From this height they could see well the flash of the machine-guns' fire on the other side of the Tancarville Canal, and hear, far up on the flat sands, the endless spitting of the cannon as the balls struck the sand. Long after the puff of white had risen, the bellow of the shot would come over the distance and move up the hill and into the forest behind, like a giant shouldering through the trees.

"If you sailed from Liverpool," said Ayton, "you came in a roundabout way enough."

"I had it in my head to go over to Ireland," said Munday, as though dreaming of it still.

He remembered very well how it was that he had walked alongside the sea looking for someplace else entirely, and standing at the edge of Liverpool with the water coming black as ink to the soles of his feet. He had not been a miser with his steps, but spent them freely toward the south, where a peasantry might with encouragement have flourished, and toward the north, where England is crowned with hills.

"Ah, did you?" said Ayton, and his face lit suddenly. "Ah, Ireland is beautiful," he said. "Dark and silent. I was a long time there. Ireland was my friend."

Munday thought of it on the other side of the water, a black jewel shining like a miner's lamp on England's brow.

"But I meant to go a much longer way," he said.

Ayton's veiled glances ran softly over Munday's face. "Yes," he said. "Yes, I know."

They were so close to the ground that the odors of what sought to grow there came to them strengthened and spiced by the wind from the sea. Ships were moving slowly up the Seine, pressing against the current of its descent, and the day was bleak; but all these things had meaning for Munday, were moving, funnel and plank, elsewhere as he himself would go.

"If a man moves east as the stars and tides do," said Ayton, "there's no harm can come to him." He drew this about him in consolation. It would stand between him and the climate of the place as no other thought could do. "It's like men being dead here in the west," he said. "It's like a man feeling when he's hungry, or feeling hurt when his bones are broke, but feeling nothing else besides. If you saw them in Borneo feeding the rice with pap as if they were human babies, and keeping the place as quiet for miles around for fear the soul of the rice be frightened and miscarry. Do you think they'd be shooting their cannon off like here if any crops were coming out of the ground?"

Below in the quarry they could see a squatter's cabin, roofed over with tar paper and tin, and a curtain of sackcloth now blowing in the doorway. A dog paced back and forth, gaunt and forsaken like the land, chained to his make-shift dog house, and the bones of his feet wearing a crescent of captivity from his wooden niche to the cabin door. However the people who had lived in the cabin might stand the weather, Munday could not determine, unless the tin pipe that stood blackened by smoke through the sandpapered roof was mouthpiece to a roaring blaze.

" 'May you be frightened neither by lightning nor by passerby,' is what they whisper to the rice," said Ayton, speaking as if the words had just been returned one by one to him in the passing wind.

"Well, how is it," asked Munday, "that now you've given up all talk of the sea?"

"Ah, I don't know," said Ayton, and his eyes went off to somewhere else. "I wouldn't say that. Maybe it's that for the time I'm sick of taking orders."

Munday sat watching a man who had come out from the squatter's cabin below and was making his way toward them up the steep land. He climbed the winding footpath with his head lowered, his body thick and tough as the root of an oak chopped off by an axe and cast out on the soil. In one hand he was carrying a swinging pail.

"There's one who takes no orders," said Munday. "Living as he likes here on the land."

"Ah, there's no style to his life," said Ayton. "You can see he's not a man of spirit. He's a squatter who has seized hold of a piece of the country, and that's no way to be. I wouldn't want to claim any part of the land. That's a woman's kind of greed. But if I had a mate to throw in his lot with me, I'd be off tomorrow, touching here and there as the fancy took me."

"You haven't much patience," said Munday. Ayton's face was turned toward him, suddenly and oddly become the face of an old man cleverly painted with-liveliness and youth. "There's one thing that holds me fast," said Munday, "and that's my piano. Like an anchor, I suppose."

The squatter had reached the brow of the hill and when the tethered goat caught sight of him she lifted her head high on her neck in alarm and flicked her tufted ears. He was coming for her, she saw in panic, and she scampered off to the end of her rope. The man was making his way toward her, step by step. Once there, he set down the pail and reached out to rope her in, but the little goat went rearing off across the barren sod.

"When a man's hard put," said Ayton, thinking of something else entirely, "then he has no choice. He has to take up anchor." They sat, watching the squatter standing with his legs spread, slowly winding the little beast in to him; first with one hand and then the other, hauling her slowly and strongly in while her glassy eyes careened in her head and she reeled on her hooves into his grasp. For all her snorting protest and the panic of her legs, her head was being bowed in submission to him by the rope that now wreathed her horns. Once he had forced her down on her knees, he held her two short ears firmly in his hand.

"Now you'll stay still," he said to her.

He kept his head turned away from the two men sitting nearby, as if they were no concern of his. The little goat butted her childish brow against his thigh, and they saw him strike her loose black lip. At this, Munday started up and walked toward him over the stiff, wintry ground.

The squatter answered Munday's question about the weather; it would probably alter in the night, he said. He stood there, planted short and soiled in his blue apron, talking with Munday and motioning down the slope to the rows of cabbages, the beet-root and the winter-salad below, explaining how it was that his crops grew sheltered on the fertile incline of the hill. His face was black with an ignorant, evil pride, thought Munday, which might with patience be exhorted from him: a man perhaps fifty, with his mustaches bristling, black and wiry, across his cheeks.

He spoke of his live-stock, and with his ruthless forefinger he raised the lip of the little goat to show them her strong yellow teeth; there was not another goat as sound anywhere in that part of the country, he said. Then he spoke of the fine sheep-dog lineage of the starving hound that turned back and forth on its chain below in the quarry. Everything he possessed he talked into a pride to himself, merely because it was his: the ugly teeth of the goat, and the bleak rows of cabbage, perhaps riddled and ravaged by slugs. He was proud to tell them how the best vegetables on the market should be tended and how celery must be spaded over to be bleached fair by the soil. When he spoke of his rabbits, he lifted his hand to show Munday and Ayton how, by striking a rabbit's neck here, in the narrow crotch where the ears were planted, the animal would be directly killed.

"Ah, that I would like to see," said Ayton, and the sound of this set the Frenchman to swelling In his shirt.

While he talked, a boy came toiling up from the quarry, and when he had reached the top he picked up the pail the man had set down and given no further thought to. As delicate as a princess, the little goat stepped to the child in obedience, and he kneeled down to milk her, to drain her tough pink teats into the pail. Munday listened to the running squirts of it, while the Frenchman told Munday that today or tomorrow maybe he was going to kill one of his rabbits. His wife would cook it in wine, he said, and when he described this the eyes of the child kneeling by the goat's side came alive. He had one brown eye and one clear blue, and the thought of eating the rabbit after it had been stewed for a morning in white wine, with slices of onion shining all around it, had transfigured his face.

On and on went the Frenchman's conceit, as if he alone was lord of the soil. His talk implied that some rare comprehension of each other's ways united him and the land. It was clear to him that no stranger could have any idea of how the earth produced, no knowledge of its accuracy and order, no patience to bear with its mysterious ways. But he himself knew all these things: knew soil and climate, was intimate with the changing seasons and equipped by his own perception to defeat the elements however fatal they might be to lesser men.

"Finish milking," he ordered the child, "and then go down without wasting any more time and feed the vines to the rabbits."

"I've fed the rabbits," said the child, getting up from his knees.

It was clear that he had no reverence for his master. But the Frenchman continued to speak of this and that with importance as he looked boldly down the land.

"We're not going to be caught unprepared again," he said in satisfaction as the cannon boomed out across the water. And it might have been himself who had given the order to fire.

"They're like as not filling orders for the tribes in mutiny in Morocco," said Munday.

But the Frenchman made as if he had not understood this foreigner's way of speaking the language, for he had no time for anything that interfered with the way his mind was made.

CHAPTER IV

T HE old gentleman could be seen through the window sitting stiff as carrion in the cold, with a muffler of blue wool knotted around his neck. On the door was hung a poster which said:

"Ancel, you have lied to the working classes!"

Not a ray of promise showed in the sky, but such afternoons of twilight were fair ones compared to the evil days of wind and rain. But wind and rain might be striking the windows forever, thought Munday, and that would never stir the old gentleman. "Under Richelieu and Colbert," Munday had read of the place, "the prosperity of the town rapidly increased." The prosperity of the town, he thought, remarking the frayed edges of the old man's coat and his eyes so red from vigilance that it seemed he must have cried for years over the exploitation of mankind. When he was young he had perhaps believed in fires built to defeat the cold, but now that he was an old man he had no time. The room was bare, but a high silk hat was on the Frenchman's head, as if to save appearances.

"Good-day," said Munday.

"Good-day," said the old man.

Surely the young foreigner who had come in was a stranger to him. But he searched the face anxiously, for he was so old now that it would be a rebuke to his faculties if he were mistaken. The face before him had a shallow layer of flesh laid handsomely over it; the eyebrows were dark, and the mouth set hard with determination.

"I've just walked over from Le Havre," Munday said, speaking his own, unhastened French. "I'd like to see the editor of the paper."

The old gentleman raised the high silk hat from his brow in greeting.

"I am Aristide Rochereau," he said. "The editor of the paper."

In Le Havre the editor of the city paper had worn a white carnation in his buttonhole. He also had a wealth of good food in him, and wine had packed its ruddy presence in his jowls. But the man before Munday was another thing entirely: a destitute gentleman, perhaps, enduring with dignity the cold outside the window and the cold within his bones, and his long yellow teeth accustomed as a rat's to gnawing cheese in solitude. Munday saw him as fatally stricken by the cold, but determined to give it no consideration. He did not have the time for it in days shaped by his trips from his home to the newspaper office by the church, defying death itself, it might be, to come and put an end to his routine.

"My name is Munday, sir," said the tall, dark haired young man. "Do you know what the fisherman do in Le Havre while they're waiting for the tide to change?"

The old man sat looking up across the mass of papers on the table into Munday's face. "No." he said after a moment. "NO." He shook his head slowly back and forth, his eyes as gentle as asters caught in the labyrinth of wrinkled brow and wrinkled cheeks.

"They stand on the sea-wall," said Munday, "and shoot the gulls down." His open hand struck the table abruptly and the old man started in his skin. "There's no reason to it!" Munday said. "The birds are shot down and their bodies float out to sea. There's no sense to it!"

Rochereau wiped the rivers of cold from his eyes and put

his silk handkerchief back into the breast pocket of his shabby coat.

"I don't believe it's of any importance," he said.

"Then you're wrong," said Munday, and he leaned over and spread his open hands on the table.

"No," the old man said, his purple lips slowly puckering. "It is of no importance. In this village," he went on, his cracked voice rising, "there is no sewer-system, no way to drain the marshes." Munday shrugged his shoulders. "These things are of importance," said the old gentleman, with his high silk hat slipped sideways on his head. "Time enough for birds," he said. "Twenty years from now. Fifty years. Five hundred years."

Munday sat down on a chair facing him, and thought of his father, remembering how he had seen him crouched behind the dunes with the snipe running out on their wiry legs and their delicate feet, to the edge of the sea. He remembered his pride in knowing that his father would never shoot a gull; of course he filled the snipe with gun-shot and they ate them, roasted brown, sixty at a sitting sometimes, their sharp wings and their breasts melting in the mouth.

"I'm an American," he said to the old man, speaking quietly now. "In America we have a law against shooting gulls."

"You have a law against drinking, too, I believe," said Rochereau. He cleared his throat and folded his mouth over and in, like a piece of crumpled linen. "There's an ammunition factory out there on the marshes," he said. "and practically every worker in it a Chinaman. Imported cheap labor while in this town hundreds of Frenchmen are unemployed. They're filling orders for dissident tribes in Morocco in order to destroy Frenchmen. Does that make sense? And you come to me talking about *gulls*," he mocked. "Ah, no! Poverty, poverty, that's what I'll talk about and I'll defeat it," he said, starved, cold bird that he was, with his beak hanging out and his head cocked to one side. He was sitting high in his chair, the worn satin buttons of his ancient coat visible now, buttoned the length of his frame. "The church," he went on, "is cold as the tomb. But the people go to it for the Sunday services and the weekly funerals and quake to the bone, coughing and spitting in each other's faces. There's foul water stagnating in the marshes under and around us,. I'm going to change all that. That's what I'm going to do." His long, bluish fingers quivered over the papers on the table. Liver spots, like little barks, had set sail across the backs of his hands. He had a peculiar dignity, a certain Spencerian contempt for anything the climate of the place might do. "In a little while," he said, "I will be mayor. When I am mayor the things I have told you about will not be. I want to be mayor in order to set things to rights. I am running for mayor on the Communist ticket," he said, and the issue of the slaughtered gulls had been set far, far aside. He took his silk hat from his head and cleaned its ancient face with the underside of his coat sleeve. "I am not a radical," he said, "but the Communist party has a local following. I chose it because it was the only platform left." He sat erect in his chair, saying, "Times have changed. In the high hat industry alone, things have changed past all belief."

Poincare's likeness lay among the papers on the table: another old man, but this one with a pointed beard on his chin, and in him flourishing the bigoted and the military age of France, the cane-cracking and the pretentious gallantry. Rochereau had drawn the photograph out to show it to Munday, and the corners of his mouth went down in sour contempt. "My father used to make all his top hats for him," he said. "He left Frenchmen sitting twiddling their thumbs in the Ruhr while England went ahead building up a labor government." Then he struck the likeness with a fillip of his long fingers, and when Poincare caved in across the middle, Rochereau thrust him into a drawer and cast a paper or two over the hostility of the Marechal's white brows.

"After the war," he said quietly, "the market for top hats never recovered. But my father left many behind." He jerked his head up on his withered neck, as if harking to some sound coming from another place, strange and far, heard by his ears alone. "Birds!" he said. "Birds! If you came out once through this town with me, that would be an end to it."

He stood up, and his livid fingers knotted the muffler close as they walked out together into the cold. An umbrella was hooked over his arm and his hat seemed to move forward in a ceremony of its own past the bleak walls. If a plague had fallen on the place, surely a greater desolation could not have been, thought Munday. There was no sign of warmth or life save for the great glowing posters of the entrance of King Carnival taking place far away somewhere in the sun. The bitter day made its way down the lanes to this sight of a painted promenade and a battle of flowers being waged somewhere in the south.

An icy sweat seemed to be oozing up through the cobble-stones from the soil, a winter sloughing of the land's foul being from which there was no escape. Further inland were the open hills where he had walked with Ayton, Munday told himself. But here they might have been miners groping in the dark for all there was any sign of the sky opening over-head.

"They want to return by some miracle," said Rochereau of the people closed away in the houses they passed. "They want to go back to what they had before the war." His voice was hushed, as if eavesdroppers might be standing behind the windows. "They don't know things can't be that way any more."

He led Munday through the foul, icy streets, this candidate for mayor of the *Cartel des Gauches* with the brown umbrella hooked over his arm, and in the heart of the town he halted, for on the stream there was a sign of life. The water was choked, without ripple or motion, although a hand-dredge, manipulated by an oarsman, floated on its surface. The man was punting and reaching like a gondolier and Rochereau watched as the refuse was stirred from the depths and followed no current, but remained static there.

"There has never been any talk," Rochereau said, "of a sewer system." He drew the back of his wool mitten across the end of his dripping nose. "They have to be given a new idea of life," he said.

On through the town they went, and at the end of it the old man stopped again and spoke of the munition factory that stood between the canal and the mouth of the Seine. Munday followed the old man's finger pointing out over the marshlands. Behind them there was no sound, no cry, no door opened or shut in the streets behind, no protest, while the sullen cannon boomed ceaselessly out on the air.

"Sugar mice!" said Rochereau in contempt. "That's what Mayor Ancel gives the children on feast-days! Sugar mice!" he said, and the tears of cold moved from wrinkle to wrinkle down his face. They walked on past the raw quarries of sand and stone set bare as skulls in the wintry hills. These places sheltered squatters, Rochereau said, and there were others settled in the marshes along the water's edge. "When I am mayor," he said to Munday, "the squatters will have to move on."

On the canal, dark and dreary boats of merchandise steamed on their way up to the port of Rouen, and there could be heard now and again the walling of a steamer as it moved out of the harbor. They were mounting the road now, and when Munday stopped for a moment to look back, he saw a heavy merchant ship quitting the locks, a ship that might be Ayton's, turning out to sea.

CHAPTER V

To step out of a door was enough to stir him; the mere thought of the air on his face and of the sky erected cloud by cloud above him summoned him from his piano-playing every day. One thing or another would draw him out, and this time it was the clear light that had fallen like a tarnished shield on the sea. As he walked to the city, he saw the waves playing across the vast expanse, back and forth, back and forth, like fingers running over the strings of a harp. He knew it was no more than the late sunlight riding the breakers, but doing so with a certain discipline, as if the high arching of them were subdued in compliance with the sun's restraint.

The gulls were flying near to the shore as he came along it. Cawing and whistling, they cavorted over the water and curved low above the darkening region of the sea. *So I see these things, sharply and clearly, disturbing my night's sleep, coming to rouse me. Feather and beak and even salt in the sea calling aloud until I start up, having been too long a time asleep.* The pale light riding on the water had now been fanned to warmth, and the sky altered, as though a fire had been kindled in the clouds. A far volcano now began tentatively to eject its rosy flakes, and a few small, sunset clouds dropped like molten lava into the sea.

But once Munday reached the harbor, the last flakes of

fire were already dying, and a shadow had spread across the sky. The water, even enclosed in the curve of the stone arms of the harbor, had turned black and evil, with every vestige of pomp and glory effaced. Down, down went the sea, sullen and bereaved of light, turning endlessly, like a dog in tall grasses, in preparation for the night ahead.

The night, thought Munday. *The black, speechless hours belong to this time, as segregation to this time. This is a time of outcasts, for such is the name given. This is the time in the century when men wander from street to street asking for understanding and, over and over, that dignity be restored to them. But the night makes no promises before going off to other places, as other continents, and man is left alone.*

Before he reached the docks, Munday knew that the *bistros* were beginning to fill with sailors come to dance with the women, for already music (if that was the name of it) was blasting on the air. The fishermen were in from the sea and climbing up to the quays with their baskets of fish hung over their shoulders. On the edge of the basin stood their wives, come out to meet them, perhaps in no spirit of welcome, but to walk them safely home; for if men lingered to themselves they would trade in some of the catch for drink or sell a good fish or two to passersby. There stood the women, determined and wife-like in their black shawls, while the sailors, with another tradition of the sea, were gathering to dance all night with the women waiting in the cafes.

They talked loudly in the doorways, their uniforms shaping their buttocks neatly and leaving their strong, bronzed necks out free.

Munday went in past them and sat down at the one empty table in the crowded place. At the other end of the cafe, a piano jangled out its tunes, and in the center, where the floor was cleared, women in brightly flowered skirts and jerseys, their feet strapped in high-heeled, champagne-colored shoes, danced around and around in the men's arms.

Munday drank down his *Pernod,* unable to give a name to the despair that now engulfed him. He sat with his hand shading his eyes while his mind pondered one thought and then the next one, seeking an explanation for why he was there. The jangling of the piano rang furiously in his ears, and the stamping of feet on the dance floor pounded in his temples. Whatever the despair was, he thought, it was not to be flogged out by any force from within. But maybe some friend would have the power to strike it down, as if it were a poisonous snake, and keep on striking with no pity for it. The separate sound of a man laughing as he danced by with a woman in his arms, even this he envied, for what friends did he have outside the Order. When the music came to a halt, he lifted his head in desperation to call for another drink. It was then that he saw Ayton coming to his table.

"I say," said Ayton, and he came to a halt before Munday. "It's a lark and a half to see you here."

Beyond them the room was waltzing and swooning in heat and chaos, but, close and clear, Munday was aware of nothing but Ayton's face. He had forgotten many things about him, he thought. He had forgotten how clear and pure the brow was, how innocent and child-like the head, crowned with its golden curls. He had forgotten the arch of the eye-sockets and the bone of the small, straight nose fitted so suavely under the skin. But he could not speak.

Then the piano set in again, and it was for a rapid, Highland fling-like dance it played. At once, voices began calling out to Ayton, and the little man buttoned his jacket over his belly and streamed out on his heels. In the middle of the place he swung his body toward the floor, his arms keeping time with the music's pace, and fitted his steps into the hornpipe of the dance. The others at their tables clapped their hands in unison to the wild beat of the music,

39

leaving the floor to Ayton alone. When it was over, he came back to Munday's table, breathing hard, and sat down.

"Did you like it?" he asked. He was as alive now as a cat in the night, his limbs turned to fire by the presence of his own kind. He sat drinking from Munday's glass of *Pernod*, his feet still dancing under the table, and he raised Munday's glass in salute to the blond girl playing at the piano, and to the others he knew as they danced by. "Next," he said, finishing the drink, "I'm going to be the archbishop and wear the red piano-cover. If only I had a seal ring," he said, and then his eyes fell on Munday's hand. It was lying on the table, the fingers held tightly in the palm as if he were in pain. "Oh, you have a seal ring, Munday!" he said. "I've always wanted a seal ring," Munday took the ring from his finger and laid it in Ayton's hand. "No," said Ayton. "No. I can't come along like a common thief and take your ring away."

Munday put out his hand and touched Ayton's arm. "Yes," he said. "There it is. It's yours." They sat silent for a moment, the smoke and music of the place drifting between them. Then Ayton lifted the ring and put it on his index finger. He made no other move but sat looking down at his hand with the slight finger burdened with the blood-red, oval ring. Then he began to speak.

"I'm going to let my ship go off without me," he said, but he did not lift his eyes to look at Munday.

"I thought you had sailed away already," said Munday, and for some reason his heart was shaking in his chest.

"Ah, no," said Ayton. The intervals of silence that came between their speech was a burden they bore in turn. After Ayton had spoken Munday could find no words to say. "If I could speak out to anyone, I could speak to you," said Ayton. "Like speaking to a man of God Almighty."

"I'm no longer a man of God," said Munday, and he held

his breath, waiting, but he did not know what he was waiting for.

Then Ayton began to speak again, and Munday heard the words uttered openly and without shame.

"Yes, you're a man of God," he said, "but in another place and time you could be a man of flesh and blood as well." Because Munday did not speak, Ayton went on saying: "The Alsatian girls are talking of going to Italy."

In his mind's eye Munday could see the south of the country as it would be, the hills strung with abandoned vineyards, left to decay years back by peasants flocking to the cities. Fleeing to Nice, Marseilles, even to Avignon, seat of the Papacy in the fourteenth century, leaving the grass to grow over the vines and the houses to fall stone by stone into decay. Down, down he travelled in his thoughts, pressing farther and farther into the land until he could picture the great rocky fists of Italy knuckling at the sun.

Yes, thought Munday sitting quiet in the heat, it would be a good thing to go to Italy. Out of the hard, indifferent heart of the north to an indolent, easy way of being. The eye would alter to the sweetness of the grapes and soften to the dark Italian skin that no hard winters came to bleach. In such a place and climate, a mistake once made would come to be a natural thing, and any shame on it would melt like the high snows dissolving.

"I'm staying ashore awhile," said Ayton, "for I can't go now. I want to be with you."

But Munday suddenly struck the table with his open hand. "To hell with you, Ayton!," he said.

He got to his feet, towering dark and sore over the smoke and the music and the dancers. For the little charity he had given, the man was taking him for something else, and he would have none of it. Not the flattery for this purpose or for any other, or his own weakness in giving ear to it, or yield to the undefinable transport of his own blood. Without another word, he flung the coins down beside the empty glass and made his way through the sailors and their women and out the door.

CHAPTER VI

O LD man Bach in his carpet slippers went clapping, tapping, jiggling around the room, stamping out on the floor the rhythm of the humble and dedicated ceremonial, bending from the hip, the neck, the knee. It was a time for music and for questioning the direction his life had taken, Munday thought, and the people who now came into his room he saw as Interlopers. Ayton was leading them, and just inside the door he set down the two valises he had been carrying. He did not advance any further, but stood there waiting for Munday to make the next move. And now Munday had ceased playing, and with one hand he indicated uneasily the chairs where they might sit, and then Ayton broke the silence.

"These are the Alsatian girls," he said, soft-spoken and humble. "Blanca, Sophia, and Annchen. They speak four languages. Did you ever hear of such a thing?"

"*Aber*, he must have heard better than that since he left the monastery," said the girl named Blanca. She was like a Rosa Bonheur stallion, it came to Munday's mind, as muscular and white as a Bonheur stallion for sale at a horse fair. And she seemed to be well-equipped with information about himself, sitting on the piano stool, he thought with some rancor; information that Ayton had doubtless provided the three of them with. "Ayton's brought some of his decorations to show you," Blanca said, and she winked her eye at Munday as she lit a cigarette.

It was clear that Sophia and Annchen dared not stray from her domain as they waited for her to look their way, to make some sign, to sit down on a chair, or walk to the window where they stood, so that they might know if they were to go or stay. But now Blanca had sat down on the floor by the warmth of the stove with her legs crossed under her, and she tossed out a handful of copper Jackmen on the boards. There she sat, playing with her Jacks and her rubber ball while Sophia and Annchen waited, their arms wound about each other, their faces turned toward Blanca's game.

"Now we should all have a glass of wine together," Ayton said. He stood hesitant a moment, his voice subdued, and Munday saw him as preparing the way, clearing it with each word chosen for a purpose, whatever that purpose might be. For what is the scene being prepared, Munday asked himself, and he watched the little man play the part so well. "I'll fetch some wine," said Ayton, and then he could keep it to himself no longer. "I have enough decorations in that bag," he said, pointing to one of them, "to keep me in comfort for life. I've got enough pipes and snow, the real kind, to put the whole city of Le Havre to sleep with dreams for a lifetime."

"*Aber*," said Blanca from the floor, not looking up. "Tell Munday where they came from." Ayton had crossed the room and taken a handful of medals from the valise, and now he spread them out on the table in the middle of the room. He stood with his eyes fixed on them, smoothing their ribbons with the tips of his fingers. This was an act between himself and the medals, an act in which no one else played a leading part.

"I won them," he said softly, "for being a remarkably brave man."

" 'Oh, ye mariners of England!' " Blanca cried out. " 'Ye

44

mariners of England that guard our native seas!' There are times," she said, tossing the Jacks out before her, "when Ayton looks like God. Like the poor little God who turned himself into a seraph and gave St. Francis the stigmata to keep him company."

The two women at the window cried out with laughter, but Munday sat silent, coming slowly to another conception of Ayton. He saw him now as a lost child. He remembered what this woman named Blanca, and what Ayton's sister, had said of him, but what they had said was no explanation for the man. They were approaching him from another direction, and whatever their words had been, they provided no name for Ayton's retreat to the sea or to his return to the land every year at harvest time. When they talked of Ayton, they had not spoken of the mystery of his quests under water, seeking some place that must be there for him, anchored and reassuring and miraculously unexplored. It was a new thing to Munday to be with people whose presence in itself did not declare their calling as did that of priests in their black skirts, or barristers carrying their fine portfolios, or sportsmen in their riding gear. But for these others, white swans, griffins, monsters, centaurs, he had become a patient sculptor, attempting to give these strangers a coherent identity. He sat at the piano, asking himself if Ayton was perhaps no more than a flash of lightning across the drab region of the north, alive and as brilliantly colored as a fox. For a moment, this was the guise Ayton took on in Munday's thoughts, but only for a moment, and then he saw him again as the lost and child-like little man.

"Let him speak out for himself," Munday said, and he might have been chastising his own condemning of others. "Let him speak before you pass judgment on him."

"*Aber*, now, Munday," said Blanca. Once more she cast out the handful of Jackmen and bounced the rubber ball.

"Don't preach the gospel here," she said. "This town's too tough. It's no place for the innocent."

The two women at the window came suddenly to life, and Sophia shook back her auburn hair and smoothed the silk of it as she looked at Blanca.

"What about mother?" she asked in a whisper. Blanca set the jacks aside and leisurely stretched out her legs.

"Well, what about her?" she said, with no interest in it.

"We promised we'd be back for a game of Solo," said Sophia.

"Maybe we will." said Blanca, and a glow was cast for a moment on the alabaster of her face and throat as she lit the second cigarette. "It won't do the old bitch any harm to wait around for a while. God knows she keeps others waiting." She winked her eye at Munday. "Ask Ayton," she said. "The first time I met him she kept us both waiting long enough."

"That was some time ago," Ayton said, and his face was flushed. "I scarcely remember." He sat down in a chair near to Munday, but he did not look his way.

"Well, just as a reminder," said Blanca. "We were waiting in line one day last year before you went off to the equator. There are always fifty sailors, or a regiment down from the Sainte-Adresse fort, or travelers waiting overnight for a boat, such a crowd waiting to get into Mrs. Sophia's house every Sunday that you have to cool your heels an hour or two in the lobby."

"I could have talked to a cat that day, just for the conversation," said Ayton in explanation of what it had been like.

"I was dressed like a gentleman myself," said Blanca, "and here was this little scamp in front of me, with no sense of humor for the situation he was in. But all he saw was my shy young face." Blanca bared her white teeth as she smiled, and fixed the two men with her bold eyes. "said Ayton to me: 'You're too nice a fellow to be waiting outside a place like this.' " Blanca slapped her knee and bent almost double in laughter. "I'd just come on the week before from Strasbourg and was sick for a sight of the girls myself."

"You've told the story so many times, to so many people," said Ayton, shifting uneasily.

"*Ta queule,*" said Blanca, and Ayton made the sign of the cross in mockery.

"I was raised in a convent," said Blanca, "and this strengthened my religious and other passions." She winked at Munday again and settled back with her feet close to the stove. "At home I had quite a following of young believers, for I have always looked upon myself as a relic, quite as authentic as a thorn from the Savior's crown or a hair from his beard. I am the reincarnation of the Nun Hadewych, the heart, the brain, and the spirit that has survived seven centuries of death. I have always made letters of prophecy in Middle Dutch, which is proof enough that the Nun Hadewych functions in my flesh, for what I know of the language is only High Dutch. In some cases," she said, "my forecasts were made in a dialect which I myself could not decipher and which turned out to be Frisian." Her story was new only to Munday and he nodded his head to her to go on with it.

"Once we were in the public room of Mrs. Sophia's House," she said, "I described this strange thing to Ayton over a glass of champagne. Two of the girls sat down at the table with us, presumably there to entice us, but all the while talking of their own feminine matters, such as velvet or toweling at how much the which, and making excursions upon our persons as carelessly as doing their nails. When the one that was to be mine, having found out that I was the opposite of what my waistcoat proclaimed me to be, she made such an outcry that Mrs. Sophia herself was called on the scene. But I had time to whisper to the young tart, 'I don't know why you're such a fool, for if you'd had the good fortune to retire with me you would not have regretted the interview.' But I was packed off to Mrs. Sophia's private quarters, and Ayton with me for having smartly slapped the Jezebel's face."

Blanca turned her head and lifted one hand to point across the room to Sophia's fiery topknot.

"To give you any idea of what Mrs. Sophia said to me," Blanca went on with it, "you must look at her daughter's hair. Surely the girl's way of looking up modestly from under her fringe was her mother's doing, but at the same time the knuckles of her hands seem to have been rapped into prominence by her mother's displeasure. The old witch spat in my eye and called me the hardest names in the French tongue," Blanca said. "And having done with that, she turned on me in my own language, which was enough to win me, no matter how viciously it was used. We were standing just inside her parlor door, and I asked her, 'Oh, *Gnadiqe Frau,* from which side of the fatherland do you come?' Her anger cooled off on hearing these words in her own language, and she said: 'I happen to come from Strasbourg.' 'Good God,' said I, 'if you'd never told me in so many words I would have known it at once from the look of intelligence in your eye! How long since you've seen the Ill and the Breusch?' I asked her. And 'how long since you were in the Munster?' she asked me. She showed us to the best seats in her neat, tasty little parlor, and Ayton and I sat down. There was a corpse in wax of the Christ-child on a table, and a bleeding heart on the mantel in recompense for the sin and wenching going on in the annex.

" 'I can see at a glance,' " said I, " 'that you are a woman of culture and discrimination.' "

" 'Oh, my library is not here for the moment,' " said Mrs. Sophia in apology. " 'My husband's family had nothing to read for the moment, so I sent it down to Auvergne.' "

" 'The dignity of deep thinking is in your bearing,' " said I, but it would have been the end if I had looked at Ayton.

" 'And when I tell you that I am a zealot of the Nun Hadewych.' " said I, " 'you will understand my mission here. I wished to impart to your young associates what portion of her mystic ecstasy my human capacities would permit, but besides this I must explain to you the plan and composition of my life.' "

Blanca turned to Munday, saying, "You, being a musician, will understand the obligations of technique. And you are also doubtless familiar with *Die Sevenste Bliscap van Maria*. But whereas the Virgin's seven joys were played upon the boards in seven successive years, I have taken a vow that my seven years, from twenty to twenty-seven, shall each one be passed in celebration of the Virgin Mary's seven joys. The first was her 'perpetual virginity' I am now, in my twentieth year, in the act of living it. For a woman is virgin as long as she is stranger to the touch of a man's hand. Next week I shall go on to her 'peculiar relation to the Godhead' which may have many interpretations, but for the present I must practice the word 'abstention' lest the sanctuary of the Lord be defiled.

"In this way," she went on with it, "I explained myself to Mrs. Sophia. But it was surely the music of her own language rather than any argument which filially persuaded her of the purity of my intentions, and she asked me who my father was. 'An electrical engineer named Schlosser," I said, 'who is making me, in the stead of a dead brother, learn his trade and work as his assistant. He has uprooted me from my native soil and brought me to this country where I'm sick for a sight of my own kind.' Mrs. Sophia took this to mean the Alsatians, and went on: 'And who is your handsome little friend here?' I took the first name that came into my head and introduced Ayton by it, for he was then a stranger to me. 'My father loves him like his own dead son,' I said, with a wink at Ayton. 'His duty is to accompany me wherever I go.' Mrs. Sophia then felt that we should meet her daughter. 'Her father was a

Frenchman,' she said. apologizing for it, 'but I have done my best to bring her up with some intelligence.'"

Blanca grinned at the company.

"When Mrs. Sophia came back," she went on, she was accompanied by her lovely daughter, looking much as you see her now: overcome with timidity, struck dumb with shyness, and fainting with humility. A gold chain around her neck bore an image of the Virgin and Child." Each word Blanca spoke became more suavely finished than the last one, as if she knew very well how deep her sarcasm could go. And at the window, the girl of whom she spoke writhed in amusement, emitting gasps of what might be described as mirth, her slender body twisting and turning with laughter beneath her fiery hair.

"I stepped forward," said Blanca, "and picked up the lifeless hand that Sophia had let fall. Mrs. Sophia then said to us: " 'The poor child has no friends at all. Of course, I do not permit her to mingle with my guests, and other nice girls of her age are, of course, kept sheltered in their homes. It is a difficult problem,' " she said to me with a sigh, arid little consideration is given to it by the general public. And she does such beautiful fancy work! Now, Sophia, show your fancy work!'

" 'Shall I show my tapestry, mother?' " asked our sweet Sophia in a swoon of timidity, " 'or the altar-cloth I am making?' "

" 'I feel sure we will pass many pleasant moments together,' " said I, pressing Mrs. Sophia's hand in mine. " 'Perhaps your daughter, ma'am, could come for an outing with us one Sunday afternoon after mass?' "

"Or after vespers, ma'am," was what Ayton now piously contributed to the conversation, and Blanca gave a snort of laughter.

"I tell you I was on the point of fumbling for my beads and beginning a 'Hail Mary,' " she began to say, but Munday raised his hand.

"Yes," he said. "Yes. Yes. Very well."

He had not yet come so far from the Church; it was still a freshly turned grave to him, still altering the look of the simplest of things. And he must stave off what more she was about to say. He sat waiting for some move to be made, and he knew that all the while he was waiting for them to go.

"I'll fetch some wine for us," Ayton said, coming suddenly to life, and in a flash he was out the door.

Here in the room the three faces of the women turned to Munday like three windows opening. *And what kind of a man are you*, their eyes were asking him, *what kind of a shadow of a man sitting there with nothing to say?* He sat silent at the piano, staring down at the ivory keys and the dark mahogany of the wood. Blanca's ball fell soft and punctual as a footstep, and the handful of jackmen rang out as she played. The tap of the ball falling and the jacks swept in and out never faltered, but now Blanca began speaking to him from the floor.

"What are you going to do about Ayton?" she asked, her voice soft and casual, nothing more than a link in the rhythm of the game.

"It's easy to see what he's done now," said Sophia.

"Yah," breathed Annchen, nodding her head. *"C'est vrai."*

Munday looked from one to the other of the women, and the two at the window clasped each other close, their faces still turned toward him.

"How will you get Ayton out of it?" asked Blanca, and she swept up a handful of jackmen and caught the ball in the palm of her hand.

"He's such a child," Sophia whispered sharply from the window, and her hands fled up to her waves of fiery hair. Her eyes were light as a goat's, and back and forth went her fringe in her uneasy fingers, back and forth like a burning fan.

"How will you get him out of it?" asked Blanca. She

snuffed out the end of her cigarette against the stove's black side. And Munday sat looking in bewilderment from one to the other: he looked into Annchen's small, terrible face, incongruous on her heavy neck, shaking and nodding like a withered flower in the wind. He turned to Sophia, smiling from the ambush of her hair, her gums out long and naked, her white, animal teeth bared. Only Blanca sat with no concern on her face. "He's up to his neck this time," she said. "What are you going to do?"

"But *me?*" cried Munday suddenly. "Why *me?*"

"He won't go off without you," said Blanca. She went on with her game. "That's why."

"Yah," said Annchen, nodding. "*Qui, vous, Monsieur Munday.*"

"It's awfully romantic, isn't it?" whispered Sophia with her naked smile.

They could hear Ayton bounding up the stairs again, and Munday turned to Blanca, seeking in her calm impersonal face some inkling to their speech. But when Ayton stepped into the room, Blanca tossed up the rubber-ball, and the two girls cried out about the weather, as if their conversation had never been of anything else.

"Oh, the rain!" cried Annchen. When she spoke one tongue, then she must repeat it in another. "oh, *la pluie!*" she must amend it. Or "*Ach, der Regen!*"

Ayton came in, wet with it, and set the two bottles of red wine down on the table. And Blanca stood up from the floor, heavy and tall, and tossed back the short light lock of hair from her face. She took the cups from the shelf above the sink and ran the water on them. *This is my house,* thought Munday, touching the keys of the piano silently, *my sanctuary, my place.* He sat watching Blanca fill the thick pewter cups with wine, filling them until they seemed about to brim over.

"What you and Ayton had better get is a change of climate," Blanca said.

CHAPTER VII

WHEN the five of them came down the hill into the quarry, the squatter's dog ran to the end of its chain, leaped high on its claws and wailed its misery aloud. Grief had given it an almost human eye, sunk deep and sorrowing in its skull, and fringed with gray. The squatter pushed aside the sack-cloth that served as door to his cabin, stepped out, folded his short, black-haired arms across the bib of his leather apron, and watched the strangers coming through the transparency of the rain.

"We've brought some friends to see you," Ayton called out. But the Frenchman gave no sign that he had heard.

Beyond the cabin stood his cart, loaded with cabbage and cauliflower, and carrots as massive as elephant trunks, tossed helter-skelter onto the shabby wagon with its shafts propped up out of the mud. Only when they stood before him could they see that there was a half-smile lurking under the dark bristles of his moustache.

"Oh, the *jolies paquerettes!*" cried Annchen.

For all it was winter, Michaelmas daisies had begun to spring up, and Annchen bent in passion over them, her fingers pinching off a white face here and there, and then back she flew to Blanca, baring the two rows of large, uneven teeth and her raw gums.

"Annchen adores nature," said Sophia.

"*Yah*," cried Annchen, nodding, and she flushed to the roots of her hair. "Cabbage, cauliflower."

"Cabbage, cauliflower," said the squatter, making it sound as if he were speaking of fine and flourishing things. But they could see for themselves the sickly, green heads of the snail-riddled cabbages, and the loose fists of cauliflower bruised with frost. Everywhere else the farmers lacked the shelter which the quarry and hillside gave his crops, he said, and he gestured with his stunted hand toward the untended stretches of land high above. "This is one of the finest properties in the Seine valley," he bragged. Throughout the beds, vegetables and flowers rambled in wild disorder, and whatever had got up courage enough to try to grow here had been strangled by the vines that overran the land. He told them his name was Quespelle, Aristide Quespelle, but he did not take the trouble to ask them theirs. He said he drove his cart, loaded with vegetables, twice a week into Le Havre in the early morning to the market place of Les Halles. In his over-weening pride in everything he possessed, he was leading his visitors to a rabbit-run, and there they halted before the glassy-eyed beasts who crouched together in the enclosure. "I might kill one of them to have for supper tonight," he said.

The long auburn face of a horse was hanging out in curiosity from its shed as Quespelle went on telling the strangers from town, from Le Havre itself it might be, that he could kill a rabbit with one blow behind its ears dealt by the side of his hand. When he opened the chicken-wire gate of the rabbit-run, the horse swung its head out of sight, and the rabbits huddled even closer together, their noses twitching, warily watching their master from the corners of their eyes. With one blunt finger, he pointed out which rabbit he intended to catch, and he set after it, as clumsy as an ox. The rabbit fled before him, now and then halting to whack a hind leg in panic on the sodden ground. Back and forth went Quespelle in pursuit, crouching low as he ran, stumbling and cursing every saint in paradise. Whenever he stopped for breath, the rabbit stopped as well, eyeing the man in panic, but no fellow beast or human being came to its aid. But by then the man was winded, and he turned in pursuit of a smaller, frailer beast that had crossed his path.

"That's not the same rabbit!" Blanca called out in icy contempt.

"Yes," Quespelle gasped as he ran, "it's the same one." The blood was beating dark in his face, and he lurched forward and closed one hand around the rabbit's ears and lifted it, kicking in desperation, in the final minutes of its life. Then he opened and stepped through the wire door and fastened it behind him, carrying the rabbit by its ears in his other hand. He was standing among them, holding the rabbit at arm's length as it twisted this way and that, like a fish caught in a fisherman's net, when he hit it squarely behind the ears with the side of his hand and they saw the rabbit's eyes turn over in his head. "*Voilà!*" he said, triumph and vanity in his voice as he held out the rabbit that had gone lax and quiet now. But after a moment, a quivering of life seemed to run over its soft, furry belly and legs. Although it no longer moved of itself, long, shuddering waves of life were breaking over it.

In a moment the man had his knife out in his hand, and he asked Munday to hold onto the rabbit's hind legs while he ripped off the skin. There were two ways of skinning a rabbit, he said, and the right way was to start under the tail and split it up to the throat. And Munday took the hindlegs of the rabbit in his two hands, and spread them wide, as Quespelle told him to. He was thinking of the Church, of the Saviour, and his lips formed a prayer in silence. *Let this last act be the release of the little creature I am holding,* he prayed.

But it was Annchen who asked if the little creature was truly dead, and Quespelle's smile again lurked under his mustache. He shrugged his shoulders, having no use for such assumptions. Munday held the two legs of the rabbit in his hands, and now he believed he could feel the life finally ebbing from the muscles and flesh. But when Quespelle set the point of the knife in at the roots of the tail, the eyes of the rabbit rolled toward them in anguish. Then it doubled over as the knife slit the length of its belly.

"Stop! Stop!" cried Munday. "My God, it is still alive!"

But Quespelle was ripping the skin off the muzzle now, baring the silky rosiness of the jawbone; but it was when he peeled off the skin from the rims of its eyes that the rabbit gave its piercing scream.

"No," said Quespelle. "It's dead. That's just the muscles tightening up." He did not look at Munday. "They always die at once if you know where to strike them, but the muscles keep on moving for a while afterwards like that," he said.

Munday turned to the others, his heart sick and fainting in him. There they stood, silenced, shocked, benumbed, staring at the man from some region of hell, and at the rabbit that he had taken from Munday's hands. And now is the time to speak, to act, Munday's faint heart was urging him, but he did not speak. Was this because for too many years the Church and his music had spoken for him, he asked himself; was this because he had, for too long a time, closed out the world of slaughtered gulls, and of rabbits skinned alive?

However it was, a woman who was a stranger to them could be seen coming up the craggy path along the bent heads of the snail-riddled cabbages. She was a young woman, wearing a man's faded work shirt that may once have been blue, and dark trousers stained darker with patches of fresh mud. Over one shoulder lay a taut leather strap that hauled a handcart of empty, ancient baskets behind her up the rocky path. Her face had nothing in common with contemporary ways or places, thought Munday, and her hair was drawn up high on her head, with a string of raffia holding it in place and the long, wavy tail of it wagging from side to side at the back of her neck. Had it been cleaner it might have been lighter in color, Munday was conjecturing as she stood among them. But even now she did not raise her eyes to them, perhaps because she wanted to be totally effaced, he thought; and when Blanca asked her name, he knew that this was true.

"I'm Quespelle's wife," she answered, almost inaudibly.

"And the boy behind you, he is your son?" Blanca suggested, but the young woman shook her head.

"He is our hired helper," she said, and she drew the boy close, as if to protect him from the unknown people gathered there.

"She's as dirty as a comb," said Sophia maliciously, but at least saying it in English.

And Annchen now gave such wild gasps of hysterical laughter that Blanca must give her entire attention to her. Both Sophia and Annchen were beside themselves at the sight of Blanca's interest in Quespelle's wife.

"*Aber, aber*, my girl, what's got into you?" asked Blanca.

But there was no way to relieve Annchen's torment. She clasped her hands together and spun around to the sight of the quiet valley below and the road leading into town.

"I say, she must be Rapunzel," Ayton said, his eyes on Quespelle's wife.

"Rapunzel, Rapunzel!" screamed Annchen, turning back to them, her bared gums livid as raw meat. " 'Rapunzel, *laissez tomber* your hair!' "

Quespelle was speaking of all there was to do before dark, and as he talked he looked at his wife in reproof that she and the child were lingering there when there were empty baskets to be filled with potatoes for the second time, and to be weighed and then stacked in the wagon, he said in irritation, and the leeks to be tied in bundles, and the rabbits were still to be fed, and the goat on the top of the hill to be milked before evening fell.

" 'Rapunzel, Rapunzel, let fall *vos cheveux*!' " Annchen cried out.

" 'Rapunzel, Rapunzel, let down your hair,' " Ayton quoted almost in a whisper, " 'so I may climb without a stair.' "

Quespelle was pointing now to the loam in the fields along the side of the canal that stretched motionless below. It was as rich as a goldmine and any crop would flourish there, he was telling them, although he had explained to them before that the farmers in the valley lacked the shelter which the quarry on the hillside gave his land.

"In another year," he was saying, "I'll spread out and plant down there as well."

He was speaking boldly of the roof that covered his cabin; next year he would cover it with tiles, and hinge a door to the place where the sackcloth blew. Sackcloth was convenient, he said, for going out and in, but a stout wooden door would serve a purpose in the winter.

"I used to be a carpenter," said Quespelle, contented to be speaking of himself. "It would be less than a half-day's work for me to plane off a solid door. But now that it's spring again," he said, shifting his feet in the icy mud, "I'll wait 'till next year before taking that on."

"If spring be January this year," Blanca said to the darkening air, "then let me pass the Ides of March in May."

Quespelle's wife had turned away to the shed and pulled open the gate of the horse's stall, and walked in to where it waited patiently.

"I used to play the trumpet," Quespelle went on with it, looking with pleasure from one face to the other. "I was a carpenter, too, a very good carpenter."

His wife came out of the shed with a pitchfork in her hand.

"Like Jesus Christ's father," murmured Ayton.

She stood still for a moment, looking at her husband. Then she turned and patted the horse gently on its rump and it shifted to one side of the stall.

"He was a *wattman* when I married him," she said.

"*Aber Gott*, what's a *wattman*?" asked Blanca in amazement.

"A man who drives a tramway," said Quespelle's wife, wondering a little at such ignorance. She looked at Blanca as if uncertain if the question were asked in humour.

"That's just what he looks like," said Blanca. "He looks exactly like a *wattman*."

With her feet in their old shoes deep in the manure and the yellow liquid of it squirting from the soles, Quespelle's wife pushed farther into the shed and began to pitch out great steaming chunks of manure. Quespelle was telling them all that his horse was greedy as a hog, and that it would eat as much as they could put in the manger for it, but still the bones would come rubbing through its hide. Not that he was underfed, but he was an old horse now, and for all they stuffed him like a sow he would never be anything but thin. "He's been eating the whole day," he said, and this over-weening for his possessions smoothed out his face. He stood watching his wife fork out the manure, her hands gripping the wooden handle of the fork as she carried the foul clots out into the barely falling rain.

Blanca looked in contempt from Quespelle's face to Ayton's, and then to Munday's, and said, "You call yourselves men!" And in her fine clean clothes and boots, she walked into the shed.

"*Deine Schuhe!*" cried Annchen in anguish.

But Blanca was stepping from side to side of the liquid straw, having taken the pitchfork from the hands of Quespelle's wife and now, faster and faster, out flew the golden globs of rich manure. From time to time, she would set the pitchfork aside and emerge from the shed with a wooden rake and gather the succulent debris into a high, pungent mound.

"It would be better to make two piles of it," said Quespelle.

"*Ta gueule*," said Blanca, and on went her strong white arms and her broad hands, pitching the straw and excrement into the open air.

The horse leaned casually against the boards of the shed, one hind foot cocked and its long face turned on its shoulder to observe them. The bony sockets of its eyes had filled with light, and now and again it shifted its weight from one hoof to another as the abomination of its bedding went flying from the shed.

When it was dark, Sophia and Annchen followed the two men into the cabin in silence, and in silence sat down to dry the soles of their shoes by the stove. The room was beginning to grow warm and a covering of yellow sand had not yet been trampled from the floor. But Blanca and Quespelle's wife had been left outside, and the two girls did not know what language the women in the shed might be exchanging, or what the dark of the horse's shed might be concealing.

Ayton as well had sat down by the stove, and now he looked at Munday and said:

"I too, I too am ready to give a hand. But which corner to turn to, where to begin tending and curing? As fast as you'd get one piece of the land repaired, the whole of it would be choked fast with weeds again. It's only the hard heart of a woman that wouldn't fail before it."

"She should do something else with her beauty, that woman, if that's the one you're speaking of," Munday said.

"Her *beauty*?" cried Sophia in derision.

"Oh, don't make me laugh!" Annchen cried out.

They sat looking in trepidation, in helpless alarm, into each other's faces; and then Quespelle came in and drew up a chair, and with both hands smoothed the rain from his hair.

"Next year I'll lay a stone chimney in," he said, but no one paid him any heed.

"One rainy night in the jungle," Ayton began, "there was Kra, the monkey, and Raong, the toad, sitting close to each other like you and me, Munday, and consoling each other. First one would complain and then the other that the weather was getting colder, pomegranates were losing their teeth from old age, and the figs were shriveling to the size of shoe-buttons. And they agreed that when the dawn came they would start making themselves coats out of the bark of a kumut tree, wooden over-coats with lizards' hides for trimming. But the next day, my dear, was bright and sunny and Kra said: 'What about those overcoats we were going to make, Raong?' And Raong said, 'To tell you the truth, you big piece of cheese, I'm jolly warm now. I'm actually in a sweat. Just touch me, I'm wringing wet, Kra-Kra.' So they played about all day, as young men will, and when the night fell Kra and Raong went under a log together and sat close to each other, like you and me, Munday, consoling each other as best they could. First one would complain and then the other that the weather was getting colder, and they agreed that when the dawn came they would start making—"

And now it was Blanca who came into the cabin, lowering her head on her strong, white neck to escape the beam of the doorway. She was carrying a bucket of coal, and she set it down beside the stove. Both Sophia and Annchen jumped up in relief at the sight of her returning to them after an hour of what had perhaps been betrayal.

"Ah, your shoes!" cried Annchen. "*Tes souliers!*"

"You're drenched," Sophia said, and she unbuckled the wet cloak from Blanca's shoulders.

"Come close to the stove, come, come!" Annchen cried out. "You've probably caught your *mort* in that filth!"

Quespelle's wife came next into the cabin, coming through the doorway in which the sackcloth hung, and Munday watched the light of the oil lamp on the table turning to quicksilver the rain that had fallen on her hair. She brought out cups of one kind and another without saucers, and a black, battered, tin coffee pot, looking at no one, as if shamed by all that was lacking, by the absence of chairs for the visitors sitting on the floor, and of rugs to cover the sandy boards.

"*Allez-oop*, the coffee on the stove," Blanca called out to her. "*Allez-oop*, the cups on the table!" From where she knelt by the stove, she reached out and caught Quespelle's wife around the waist. "What about *your* shoes?" she said. "Doesn't anyone see that you don't catch your death?" Sophia and Annchen sat watching and harking, shaken by what was or was not taking place. "Come here and let me take your shoes off," said Blanca gently. But Quespelle's wife had already freed herself from the other woman's arm, and was bringing out the goat milk for their coffee and a loaf of dark bread as well.

CHAPTER VIII

No word was said, no sign given, but when the time came Munday and Ayton, as if it had been agreed on beforehand, were the first to leave the cabin and the quarry and walk down the road, but walking separately, like strangers in the dark. But Munday knew very well, as though a light were shining on him, the look and the gait of the man walking on the other side of the road. He knew well how he looked when he turned his face to woman or man and embraced them with his speech. Such was his regard, given to everyone without economy, cheap as spinach. Such was the attention and such the compliments that Ayton's eyes and tongue squandered on anyone who happened to come along.

Soon I shall have it out with him, thought Munday. It would not be long now, for a just wrath was consuming him. How he would begin to speak he did not know, for his passion had no name to it, but its clarity was as good as a cloak drawn around him, keeping the chill of Ayton's idle talk away. A little bit here and another there, he thought, was how Ayton disbursed his substance. He wanted no explanations from him, for Ayton's concept of truth had many faces. He wanted no "this I've done," or "that I tried not to do."

"It may be well enough in your early youth, Ayton," he said across the dark barrier of the night, "to live as you do without any thought for anyone else, or without storing your strength away against a time of need." Although there was no way the eye could see, he believed the other man's troubled face had responded to these words. "But what becomes of a man if he doesn't keep something in himself strong and everlasting?" Munday asked.

"Ah, that I don't know," came Ayton's voice, almost tragically, from the other side of the road.

"There's an obligation a man owes to dignity," Munday went on saying, and again it could have been his own soul he was exhorting. "A man can move from one thing to another and not be destroyed as long as the lives and the hopes and directions others have taken are as important to him as his own." But all the while he might have been giving himself counsel, curbing his own envy for this little man who could go heedlessly whichever way he willed. "But someone like you, Ayton," he said, "you give your friendship lightly, and I suppose take it away in the same manner. You give it to this, that, or the other one," he said, and then he began to fear that the other might in some way mistake his fervor. "Of course, it's of no great importance to me," he said, "but I can't bear to see any man wasting his substance, squandering his own being on any casual encounters that happen to come along."

"I never thought it was of any importance to you," said Ayton. "I never thought you cared what I did."

His voice was humbled and quiet still, but Munday believed he could hear a muted note of celebration in it.

"You're no more than a stranger to me," Munday said, "but the first night I saw you, you came to my room asking for help, and the only help I can give you, if such you can call it, is the truth about yourself. You came seeking a stranger to get you out of trouble, and I am still a stranger, for I do not know to this moment what your trouble is. You came to me for comfort, and not for confession, and the only comfort I could ever see for a man's soul is the truth wrung out of him, no matter how it may sound."

"This way, without seeing your face, I could tell you the truth, I'm sure," said Ayton. He spoke so softly that Munday must strain his ears to catch the words. "I'm sure I could make everything clear to you," Ayton said.

"But no," said Munday. "I want no confessions from you. I'm not a prophet dispensing salvation." The night lay motionless all about them, on every side. Whether it was the rain or the invisible mist that blotted out direction, the darkness was impenetrable and silent except for their own steps giving purpose to it and their two voices echoing in the damp cave of the night. "There's no reason why you should tell me anything," he said. "There's no cure or explanation for anything that's happened outside yourself. You know nothing at all of me or what I am, but still you'd come to me and deny your own sister, and you'd sit down with a family of squatters unknown to you and speak out, just for the waggery of doing it, against your own kin. Or you'd kiss the cheeks of the Alsatian girls, openly, yes, it is true, as a child might, but there'd be more sincerity to it if you kissed them in secret."

"Ah, don't worry your head any more about me," said Ayton softly, but for a moment Munday heard an echo of triumph in his voice diminishing the sound of pain.

"But why is it they come to me, these women," Munday said to him then, "asking me to hold out a helping hand to you?"

"There's always a woman somewhere," said Ayton, "ready and waiting to give a man away."

"No," said Munday, "That's not the question. But I tell you, you must have something to give your life a shape or else it's a burdensome thing that you'd be well rid of."

"Ah, I've often thought of ridding myself of it," Ayton said.

"I'm not recommending that to you," said Munday from

the side of the road he walked on, while on the other side walked Ayton, and it was as if the dark between them were never to be spanned. "There's no reason for me to be preaching to you as I am, except that I've abstained for so long now," said Munday. "It's scarcely my place to go about now saving souls for God, but I would help any man to save his own, if I could do it."

"You'd be wiser to just turn your back on me and pay no heed," said Ayton in his gentle, grieving voice.

In a while, thought Munday, they would come into the city, for lights were springing up now like dim stars in the heavens, and Ayton would take one street and go in that direction, and he would take another and go a different way. Even in the darkness, it seemed to him that he could see Ayton's nimble legs in motion, and hear the small feet following each other in an almost musical rhythm. No other being he had ever seen possessed this andante-measured step, unless it was a group of foreign negroes seen passing on the docks of Le Havre one day. He had watched them crossing the stones of the wharf, supple and delicate-limbed men, as gentle as deer, with their proud heads lifted, antlering the cold.

"I heard these men speaking among themselves," said Munday, thinking aloud about them. "They talked a language that went, like music, lackadaisically from lip to lip. They weren't made for the place. They had no bold front to cope with it, yet nobody passing saw them as any different from what ordinary Frenchmen are. I followed them and they stopped at one shop window in the city, the sight of checkered, automobiling caps stuck there on the wax heads of white models. They couldn't bring themselves to move on for a while because they wanted so badly to have the caps for themselves."

"A woman," said Ayton from across the road, "would be blind to anything like that."

"You can't lay the blame for every fault on women," said Munday in irritation.

"Ah, yes," said Ayton, but he spoke in humility, as though he would not willingly disagree. But the truth was forced from him and he could not deny it. "Women have been kept to themselves, always, with simple, natural instincts. Even the Indians," he said, as if it all grieved him, but so it was. "Whenever there was a festival, the men swept the sacred squares clean and kept the women and animals off them. They are impure," he said gently. "Yes, they are impure."

"What of the Virgin, then?" Munday asked. But even as he spoke he knew, as he had always known, she had no place with the Trinity, and that her presence in the Church embarrassed the holy there.

"Oh, the Virgin corrupted all women," said Ayton, quietly, "by bringing them into prominence."

"She came into the Church through no will of her own," said Munday, listening for the sound of Ayton's footsteps as he spoke.

"Ah, you're an educated man," Ayton protested, but whether his pious voice was mockery or not, Munday did not know. "There may be other explanations found in books, but as long as I've lived I've never found a better."

"You've done quite a bit of reading yourself," Munday said. "I've been wondering how you had the time for books in the sea-faring life you led."

"I had a friend who was a traveling librarian all over Lancashire County," said Ayton, and there was a sudden eagerness in the sound of his voice. "We got acquainted when my ship tied up in the Glasgow harbor, and I was with him a solid two years, Munday, and we'd spend all day and half the night reading the books he handled."

"That must have been very interesting," Munday said pleasantly enough, but a surge of holy wrath was rising in him.

"His name was Macleod, Ian Clancy Macleod," Ayton went on with it, speaking as if from a dream on the other side of the road. "He was a writer as well, so perhaps you've heard of him. He wrote a book called *The Golden Bough*."

"Oh, come now, "Munday said in protest. "That was written by a man named Frazier. He was from Glasgow, that's true, but he was never a librarian."

"Ah, that needs explaining. It's a sad enough story," Ayton said. "Macleod wrote the book fairly and squarely, and Frazier took the credit for it. That was what broke my friend's heart."

"Oh, come off it, Ayton!" Munday almost shouted the words across the road. "You fell for a cock-and-bull story your fine friend was feeding you, knowing you'd fall for it in your innocence!"

"He was a very handsome man, Macleod," said Ayton, his voice still grieving for him. "He was well-built and dark-haired like you, Munday, only you are the handsomer of the two."

Now they had come to the road, and in the pale lights from the street-lamps, Munday could see the little man striding strongly and sensuously on, like a man hastening secretly, but with all his flesh in declaration, hastening to nameless, wild delights. They were coming near to the end of the street, and here it might be, thought Munday, here it might be that Ayton would turn off toward his own quarters. Here it might be that the child-like little Englishman, riding the power that his thighs clasped like a mount beneath him, would take his departure. Here he might leave him, Munday thought, and a surge of holy wrath engulfed him.

"What kind of life of abomination do you live?" he cried out. "What kind of evil are you trying to force on me?"

Ayton walked on in silence for a moment, and then he

said, "Munday, I left my valises in your room. I'll have to go and fetch them, if you wouldn't mind."

"Yes," said Munday, and he felt suddenly relieved, for now the decision need not be his own.

"Now that I see how you feel," Ayton was saying, "I'll take them elsewhere."

"But if you had thought to leave them there for a while with me," said Munday, "there's no reason to carry them off so fast."

"Yes," said Ayton, "Now that I see how I seem to you, I won't stay another night in the city."

"What of your sister?" Munday asked.

"It doesn't matter," said Ayton.

There in the room the book Munday had been reading in the morning lay open on the table. And now he put his hand on the page and stood reading over and over the words that were written there: " . . . the choir, because he built out even more boldly to the east than to the west, fell in 1421 after four hundred years of life."

Ayton had picked up his bags, but he waited, hesitant.

"Well, good-by, Munday. Well, I'll be off," he said.

"You'll go to your sister, won't you, then?" asked Munday, turning away. *The choir,* he was thinking in his distress, *as strong and impregnable as granite, it fell in 1421 after four hundred years of inviolate life.*

"No," said Ayton. "God knows what will become of me. God knows where I'll go." Abruptly he set down the bags and took a few steps toward the other man, but now Munday had crossed the room to the piano. These things stood between them, he knew: the music, the books, even the Church, and these were the things that must remain unshaken. "It isn't right for me," Ayton was saying. "It isn't right for me to be going off without you."

But Munday's fingers moved in their own separate life on the keys. Ta-ta-de-dum, said the piano gravely.

"That's the song of Mont St. Michel," he said as he

played, and for a while Ayton stood quiet, listening. But only for a while, and then he repeated:

"We could go there together, we could go off together to Mont St. Michel."

"You've gone off too many times," said Munday.

"But never with you," Ayton said.

"No, never with me," said Munday, still playing, but he knew that the power of music was crumbling within him, as had the power of the Church. He was shamed by this revelation, and the perfidy of his own preaching, but he knew that it was too late to falter, for if he faltered now his own pride would be shattered. "I don't like to think of you as having no discrimination," he went on saying to the accompaniment of the music. "You've gone off in your life with too many people. I'm aware of that. You have no pride," he said.

"But a strong man," said Ayton, "could teach me pride." Munday sat playing, seeking courage from the pure flight of the keys. "I want to be saved!" Ayton cried out, and he fell down on his knees beside Munday. "I can't be damned forever! I'm not an evil man! I have to be saved from myself, and it's only you can save me. I want to be with you always. I want to live my life with you!"

"How many times have you said that before?" Munday asked, his voice as if strangled in his throat; and now he stopped playing.

"But never to you!" cried Ayton.

"No, never to me," said Munday. "But now you have said them to me, Ayton, now you have said those words to me."

He saw the little man's face turned up to him in homage, in wonder, almost in innocence, and he held out his hands to him and followed where he led.

CHAPTER IX

B UT immediately the hand of Edith Ayton was as good as raised between them. Munday could see it clearly, with the queer old ring on the finger and the freckles across the back of it. It shook in menace at them when they sat down to coffee in the morning. It threatened them in rebuke for the intimacy and passion of the night.

Munday saw himself now filling the role of the third one, always a third one, who wound rend brother from sister. In other times and places it had been other people, but now it was himself, a stranger like all the others, who was fated to be the villain of the piece.

"What will your sister do now?" he asked.

Ayton looked up, so tender, so young, with his hair combed back, shining like gold, from his brow.

"I haven't any sister," he said. "I made her grow out of a flower-pot, by my own magic, for a purpose. I mean, the way the fakirs do. She isn't really there." But down the stairs her hand was in pursuit, and it followed them around the harbor. "She grew up like an orange tree, and produced only withered, effeminate blossoms, and sour, rotting fruit," Ayton said.

As they skirted the water, Munday saw the green of the land-locked tide, more wondrous than it had ever seemed to him before. There are some, he thought, whose lives, and whatever action they take, are sanctioned by beauty, and this man's life is so, and there is no way to explain it. His holy beauty could almost make a saint of him, if he wished, for it a belt of, yes, chastity of the spirit. But the hand of Edith had closed into a fist that sought to strike the two of them.

"Well," said she, out of breath as she halted before them, "I've had a fine time looking for you two. I've been up those flights twice and down them again. Didn't Ayton tell you I was coming along for my lesson?"

Munday reached out in mock bewilderment and touched her sleeve.

"Are you substance?" he asked her, and Ayton burst into laughter.

"Substance I am!" she said, and a red flag of outrage was waving in her face. "Substance, as hard as rock." She pointed her feet out sharply before her as she walked, the toes first to the right and then to the left. "Substance, substance," she said, and now the three of them had reached the city street. "Wherever you happen to be going, I'm going right along." She took a few grim, glancing looks at herself in the shop mirrors they passed, and thrust back the locks of her grey, rebellious hair. "Whether I'm wanted, or whether I'm not," she said, "I'm going right along with you. After all, I'm your pupil, Mr. Munday. I have some sort of claim."

It was a mild morning, with a velvety fog almost blotting out the open sea and, wary as cats, cab-horses came stepping out of the mist and over the cobbles, as if each step into obscurity might be their last.

"What a climate!" said Ayton. "The sooner I'm out of it the better."

"I dare say," said his sister, but the little man paid no heed.

"This time last year I was on the Mediterranean," he said to Munday, "and the fish even were nosing around, trying to find a cool place under the shadow of the ship." He

72

looked at his sister. "One day we hauled in an octopus," he said brightly, "and the anger of the lady! She bumped up and down on her bottom until she was blue in the face, and beat the deck with her fists, hundreds of them, in fury. Such a sight!" said Ayton, speaking without a trace of malice. "Shreds of her hanging exactly like hair over her mug, and those elongated bits of her suddenly growing curious and sticking out of her hide like so many telescopes fixed on you."

"I dare say you couldn't stand anything like that," said Edith savagely.

But she put her venom aside for a moment when she saw that they had hailed a street-car at the corner, and she climbed in after Ayton and sat down. There sat the three of them, riding out from the city, and Munday with no thought for her because of this thing that had blasted the very foundations of his life. Here he might sit, seemingly like any other man seated on the wooden benches of the trolley, but the disparity was too great to be defined. Should he feel himself set apart from others by sin and abomination, he asked himself, for these two words referred to the act, but they did not persuade him. They could not describe the drama that had been enacted in his flesh. *Abomination*, he repeated to himself, but his heart was brimming with wonder; *abomination and sin*, he said, seeking to give them meaning, but the glamor remained untarnished, undefiled.

When the car halted in the little town, the three of them descended. Munday had in his pocket the protest he had written out for the slaughtered gulls. But he might have been moving in a dream, first past the portals of the church, and then to the steps of the editor's office, with the two others following behind. Only when he thought of Ayton did his mind ignite. The fire of it was there, even in his guilt and his confusion, consuming the residue of all that had gone before, endowing him with a new manly power.

Rochereau opened the door to them, cocking his head and harking in the cold. He led them into the room in ceremony and placed a chair for the lady. His silk top hat sat on a chair in one corner of the room.

"Cold," shuddered Edith, nursing her arms and the wounded heart in her bosom.

"Cold?" asked the old man. He spoke the word as though it were new to him, and a light of buffoonery came into his eye as he went to the cupboard. "I have a little bottle of cognac that might warm us," he said, and from the gleam in his eye he could have been leading them into some kind of mischief. He took out the small, stemmed glasses from a shelf, and filled them carefully, one by one. "Mr. Munday," he said, "I've kept half a column open for you in the paper."

"Oh, my!" cried Edith in derision. "Are *you* getting involved in it Mr. Munday? What are ye anyway," she asked. "An artist, a musician, a writer, a philanderer, or what?"

The old man bowed to her as he lifted his glass, one hand placed elegantly away under the tails of his worn coat.

"Mr. Munday is an American," he said mildly, "educated in England, living from choice in France."

Edith gave a snort of laughter.

"What?" she shouted. "That has nothing to do with it. He's a musician!" Her hands galloped up and down before her on imaginary keys. "The piano!" she shouted. She looked ready to strike him with her raised hand.

"Yes," said the old gentleman, bowing, "but when there is poverty, hunger, disease among the less fortunate—"

He unwound the scarf from his throat and set it aside.

"I've written about the gulls," said Munday.

He took the pages from his coat and laid them on the table.

"It's a beginning," said the old man, but a look of regret had crossed his face. "They are not a necessity—"

"And what about your high silk hat, then?" cried Edith. "What's that got to do with the cause of the people?"

He stared relentlessly at the posters on the wall. Her heart was sore, so she must strike out like a wounded snake.

"*Ancel, vous tremblez!*" said the posters, and her mouth turned down in contempt.

Only Ayton possessed sugar sweet enough to drop word by word into the sour brew of her presence, but his mind was elsewhere, paying heed to Munday's face, or to Munday's words, and he did not speak.

"For the time it can't be anything but the gulls," said Munday. He thought of the mean, venal look of the Frenchmen who had ridden in the street-car beside them, and there his patience halted. He had come this far for the sake of the gulls, and for nothing else. But he said, "And I wanted my English friends to meet you."

"England," said the old man. "What a proud name!" He lifted his glass and sipped a drink to England; for England, he said, had done things politically very broadly and well. And Englishmen had no interest in money, none at all. The French were misers, the Italians greedy as children, the Americans were too far away. "This is the first drink I've had in years," he said. The strength of it had stained his cheeks, and he reached for the chair under him and set himself carefully down. He seamed his old mouth tight across his face and looked waggishly at Munday. "The last time I drank cognac," he said, "was when Lyautey resigned as Minister of War. I got into trouble for my satisfaction over that," he said. "My piece came out in the paper next day and the Royalists came over to pay me a call with a collection of canes that would have done any dandy proud. Some of them, boys back from the front on sick-leave," he said, "and one of them in particular a young man I had

75

reason to know very well." His cheeks hung down as empty as the jowls of a blood-hound, and his hand shook like an old woman's on the buttons of his coat. "How times have changed!" he said with a fragile laugh. "Dear, dear, Munday, I must be getting old." He leaned over the table and put his hand, knotty and gnarled as the bark of a tree, on Munday's arm. "Or perhaps the cold. Age or the cold. One or the other, or perhaps both." He looked up startled at Ayton, who, for the second time, was filling the little glasses to the brim. "Is it cold in here?" he asked. Then he turned his afflicted eyes again on Munday. "You," he said, with his smile set askew under his nose, "you might very well be my son, you know. But, imagine me, father to a fine young gentleman." He reached for his glass and sipped it slowly. "He had a smart coat on and a flower in his but-tonhole, and white gaiters over his shoes. He walked right into this office without so much as a rap on the door. I was sitting here at this table, and he walked in with half a dozen other young men behind him. He strutted right up to where I was working, with his hat cocked on one side of his head, and he said to me: 'When you wrote what you did in your paper this morning, Mr. Rochereau, you forgot about the *Action Française*.' And without another word," said Rochereau, "he leaned over this table and slapped my face." The old man put his hand to his cheek as though he still felt the smart of it. " 'It's men like you,' said this infant to me, 'who would make a Russia out of France!' I jumped up and I ordered him and his lot out of the office. A man of sixty-five," he said wistfully, "speak-ing his mind out to these young dudes and dandies! 'If you don't know where my sympathies lie,' said I, 'then read my editorial written the day after the Petrograd garrison went over to the people!' His answer to this was the crack of his cane on my shins." Rochereau managed to laugh out loud now, but his old eyes were streaming when he turned to the strangers in the room. But there was no sorrow in his voice, only a far echo of courage or endurance that Munday could not find the word for. "That was my son," he said. "That was my son," he repeated, and he took a handkerchief from his coat pocket and blew his nose. "That was my son, and I lifted a chair over his head, but the crowd of them took it away from me. One of them gave me a blow on the chest that I'll take to my grave. They broke every window in the room, and I trying to hinder them, and when they had laid me out on the floor, they packed my books and papers into the chimney and set fire to them. That was my son," he said once more. "But I can't blame him." His voice was high and faint now. "He didn't know."

CHAPTER X

W HEN I first met that young gentleman's mother,"
Rochereau went on saying, "it was before the time
when they began making high hats out of calico." He was
lost to them now, lost in the far place of his youth, with
the cognac urging him on. "That was the best time," he
said. "That was before the decline in manufacturing set in.
I was the head of one department in my father's factory,
and I had my inspection tour to make every morning to
see that the brims of the hats were well polished and
curled. I lived alone with my father and did as he bade me,
but he always allowed me a bachelor room of my own
where I had the books and whatever adventures I pleased.
More books than adventures," he added, "because women
were always a mystery to me. There wasn't a volume of
Zola to be found in my father's library, but I read him at
night in my own room. And one morning when I was on
inspection a young girl on the bench ran a needle of one
of the machines into her forearm. I was there by chance
when it happened and I kept the poison from her blood
by pressing my mouth to the wound and sucking it from
her. She told me her name was Mado, and ever after I took
the habit of talking a good part of the day with her. I explained to her the mechanism of the revolving machines
on which she worked, and we leaned over the rollers,
watching the wheels slip into each other and give the hats

their glossy finish. Our friendship seemed destined to grow into something stronger, but she told me she was engaged to marry a young journalist, a man so superior to herself in every way that her mother had seen a brilliant future for Mado in such a match. "This girl," he said, abruptly losing his patience, "was nothing but a child. She was just seventeen and certainly did not know her own heart. But here she was being whipped into a marriage with a blue-stocking and a scamp. When I told her as much, she burst into tears and confessed she had no affection for him. But she had given her word to marry him as soon as he had an increase in salary. I told her she could not marry a man she didn't love, for I felt that as she was in my employ she was, in a sense, under my protection. 'I have only one word,' she answered me, 'and I have given it.' I was outraged by her heartless determination and went so far as to reprove her for her light ways. The poor child was distressed by this and mistakenly stitched the upper brims on a dozen or more high hats where the lower brims should have been. The next day these hats were caught up by my father and he called me to his office to reprimand me for having let them pass. I took her part, but no matter how I explained it, my father was convinced Mado was a loose woman because of the black curls she wore long in her neck. I told him that it was her mother's obstinacy that kept them there, and he said perhaps it was her mother's obstinacy as well that made her wear to work stilt heels and dresses cut low in the front like a ball-gown. I was so angry that I was trembling. My father said my attempt to champion the lower classes was no doubt admirable but in spite of it this young woman must lose her place. I went hastening down to little Mado's bench, and I said to her: 'Put on your bonnet, Mado, and take my arm, for the two of us are leaving this stronghold of the Pharisee.' "

His eyes had scarcely moved from Munday's face as he spoke. They were turned toward him as though to a shining light. For Munday sat silent, listening in compassion to him, while the brother and sister could never lay down their arms.

" 'And a man shall be as a hiding place from the wind,' " Ayton was saying softly, " 'as a covert from the tempest, as the shadow of a great rock—' "

"Ah, yes, I daresay!" said Edith sharply.

"Then what happened?" Munday asked Rochereau, urging him on even as the Church wooed the uneasy to speech.

"She stood up beside me," said Rochereau, "and tied her bonnet under her chin and she walked bravely out with me through the workroom, holding with both hands to my arm. I led her to the public gardens, and there she sank down on a bench and began to sob. 'If my father cuts me off for this,' I said, 'I can surely make a living elsewhere.' She accepted my proposal of marriage and fell weeping on my shoulder. She could not return to her home, she said, for her mother would oppose the two of us. 'So much the better,' said I. 'I'll take you to my bachelor room where you can remain in peace and quiet until I have the license. I can easily find a bed for myself in a nearby hotel.'

"I took her to a respectable restaurant I knew of, overlooking the cemetery at Sanvic. The gates of the cemetery were still open and Mado felt that after dinner a walk through that quiet place would restore her peace of mind. She hung on my arm as we made our way through the graves, and the sight of a young child's, with its wire cage of wax angels and photographs of the little dead soul were enough to send the poor girl off into another spasm of weeping. 'Why is it we all must die?' she asked me. 'Why must we die? Couldn't a difference be made,' she kept saying, 'for you and me? Or anyway for me?' I took out my handkerchief and wiped the tears from her lovely face. I asked her to give me the happiness of hearing her call me by my name. And then to my own surprise I found that

I was embracing her, or rather that we had, with no intention of doing so, fallen into an embrace. I had ordered a bottle of wine at dinner and we had finished it, and I am sure it played its part in altering the natures of two shy people. Do not misunderstand me," he said hastily to Munday. "It never occurred to either of us to sleep under the same roof. We drove to my quarters in an open carriage, and I was content to sit beside her, keeping out of sight, under my briefcase, my hand that was holding hers, for I wanted no casual passerby to witness this evidence of our affection. And Mado was so cool and distant during the drive that I knew she shared my feelings. She counted the stars coming out above us, and under the light of every street-lamp she turned her head away from me. I sent the vehicle off at the door, for the hotel I had in mind for myself was not far distant. After I had shown her up the stairs to my bachelor quarters, I was prepared to take my leave. I hoped to leave without having to raise my eyes to hers, for I feared what that might lead me to do. 'I shall be back early in the morning,' I told her, and then Mado suddenly flung herself on my breast. 'I can't sleep here alone!' she cried. 'I'm too afraid of the dark!'

"I awoke in the morning," Rochereau went on with it, "and Mado was still asleep, with her head on my shoulder, and her high-heeled slippers standing side-by-side on my writing desk. I looked a long time at her face," he said, "and it was well I did, for I never saw her again, never at any time, never anywhere." His mouth was like a string drawn taut across his withering face, and his voice faltered. "I never saw her again," he murmured. "She went home after breakfast to gather up her clothes, and I went off to the *Mairie* to arrange about our marriage. When she didn't come back by nine at night, I went to her mother's door and knocked. 'I'm Mado's employer,' I said, 'I want to see Mado.' I imagined I saw Mado's face crying for me in every window of the house. 'So you're the young scamp!'

said Mado's mother. 'Well, I got the best of you, even if you did keep my daughter out all night. She went off to Paris this afternoon with her fiance, and they'll be married at once.' She closed the door in my face and that's all I ever knew. Whatever else I heard about Mado was from my father. After a while I swallowed my pride and went back to work again. And one night he told me the name of the journalist. There was an article in the paper with his name to it. 'That's the man they married Mado off to,' my father said. And in another few months he showed me something else in the paper. 'That journalist Mado married,' he said, 'has just had a son.' I jumped up from my chair at the dinner-table and threw down my napkin. 'That's a lie!' I said to my father. My father stood up, too, and he put his arms around me, and he said, 'It isn't a lie, it's true.' I sat down and I began to cry in front of my father. I don't know what it was, except that he had never before put his arms like that around me. 'It's not his son,' I told him. 'It's mine.' My father walked out of the room and we didn't speak of it again. We never made any mention of it," Rochereau said, "but my father didn't forget that night any more than I did. He knew what it was that kept me forever from marriage, and he knew too how bitter it was for me to know my own son was growing up a Royalist and not a drop of Royalism in his blood. That was the young dandy," said Rochereau, trying to find some humor in it, "with Mado's little face attached to him, and her eyes and hair, he was the one who came over and slapped me. The first time he hit me, I could have sworn it was Mado leaning over this table here to hit me in the face."

The old man leaned back in his chair, perhaps trying to laugh, but at the same time wiping the tears from his cheeks with the back of his hand. Edith had pinned back the straggling, grey locks from her brow and she sat shrewdly eyeing him.

"With all your pretentions to this and that," she said, "you got what you wanted from the poor, innocent girl."

"Eh, what was that?" said the old man, returning to them. "Eh, eh?" he said, as though he had not heard her well.

But before she could speak again, Ayton had jumped to his feet and faced his sister.

" 'A man shall be as rivers of water in a dry place!' " he cried out. "Can't you understand what this man is saying to us? If you had ears to hear, you would hide your head in shame," he said. "But it's a curse on you, being a woman! A woman can never be any of those things is what this man is telling us. You can never be 'a river in a dry place, or a hiding place from the wind, or a covert from the tempest' . . ."

CHAPTER XI

W HEN Munday and Ayton had stepped off the toy
train with its puffing engine, Ayton ran quickly
out over the sands toward the disappearing ocean. Endless
beaches, one after the other, paved the way to the receding
water, and to either side of the expanse of sand stretched
the black woods of the mainland. Above them, high and
perilously clear against the January sky, the church stood
deep and tall, out of reach from the tides and fortified by
the warriors' wall that flanked the island. It was strange
to Ayton, but to Munday it had been long before perfectly
drawn and detailed, like a dry-point in his heart.

He remembered well the first trip he had made to it,
coming straight to the Mont from England, he himself a
mere child walking with Bishop Rosencrans who had
given him this holiday to pay homage to the Virgin. She
stood alone, with her face black as pitch, tender and youthful, but ready at any moment to pacify the monstrous tide.
She was a Moorish Virgin left behind and enchapelled,
held as a hostage almost, by the monks who fought like
warriors for their belief.

Among Munday's papers there was still the composition
he had written before sailing from England and it had begun: "One dull June morning as we were stammering
through a somewhat difficult passage of Virgil in our large
classroom, we were startled by a knock at the door, fol-

84

lowed by the page who announced a visitor for 'Master Munday'—me! You can imagine what a bound my heart gave, for I quickly surmised a visitor from home, and the hope of meeting a familiar face after eight months of estrangement from all friends was joyous indeed. I need scarcely describe my delight at meeting again dear Bishop Rosencrans, with his bright, smiling face, and listening to that voice so well-known of old, sweetened this time with the gladdest of tidings from my distant home."

As if he could reach its far diminishing edge, Ayton was still hastening toward the ebbing water, and Munday stood alone at the threshold of the town, as he had stood as a boy, waiting for the Bishop to settle where they would lodge. In the afternoon the Bishop had kneeled down in his black skirts and dropped shells and the heads of flowers into the pools of quicksand among the rocks. For a moment the shells and flowers had quivered on the surface of limp sand, and then sunk slowly out of sight, while the Bishop questioned Munday about his school.

"Never any unpleasant incidents, Munday? I mean between the boys, you know?"

He could hear the Bishop's warm, winning voice speaking now as it had once spoken.

"No, no, never anything, sir," said the child's voice, bewildered, but not daring to ask any questions. He had shown the Bishop every corner of the English school on the day before they left. "First we conducted him through our new school dedicated to St. Lawrence; everything was inspected, the dormitories, classrooms, library, refectory, and finally the parlor; then we entered the sacristy and Father Manning exhibited to him our great reliquary case, the richest in England and rivaling many in Rome." So he had written of it, but even then he knew that he had hurried the Bishop past the cloister. Bishop Rosencrans had not seen everything. The stone bench had not been pointed out to him where, on such a dull English morning, Munday had seen in passing the bodies of two young boys lying in its shadow, locked singularly in embrace. Was this the "unpleasant incident," this overwhelming sight? It had taken the strength from his knees and sent him reeling down the hall.

"After the sacristy came the church itself, cold and bare indeed," he had written later, with plain white-washed walls and unornamented roof, yet possessing no less than seven altars, with their peculiar privileges, and all of them laden with indulgences and Papal favors. Adjoining the church is the Community House; here the Oblate Fathers met the Bishop in the Reception Room. After a short stay his Lordship accompanied us to the Oratory where we sing the Office of the Blessed Virgin on Sundays and Feast-days. Here under our little altar is preserved the body of St. Clement, enclosed in wax, a boy martyr supposed to have died for his faith when only ten years of age."

It was the memory of this boy that now filled Munday with anguish, knowing that it was such a child who had walked the long way through Brittany to come to the Virgin in worship. He stood below the stone arch of the entryway and looked up at the town to the Mont. It was all so well-known to him, the walls, and the roofs, and the stone stairways in place of streets. Like winging eagles, the flying buttresses sprang from the church's side and arched out toward the needle trees of the mainland. Every separate act of his life, Munday knew, had served to shape the armor of St. Clement's wax that kept from outrage another boy's flesh and bone. His life of high purpose, both the church and his music, had modeled within him the sweet, passionless face of virtue that he had believed could preserve forever from sin the slight figure that had kneeled down beside the Bishop at the Virgin's feet.

Was it in this way, he asked himself, that women mourned their lost purity? He could not recall ever having seen it in the faces of any women, a grieving over the assault upon the undefiled maiden each of them had been. But his love and his grief for the child who had accompanied Bishop Rosencrans to the Mont now drew him off to the Virgin's chapel, that he might visit it alone. All the miraculous purity of his years came hopelessly, helplessly to him. What purpose had it served if he had yielded in the end? He remembered St. Aloysius' House with such clarity that he could not bear to set his foot on the first step of the chapel. To St. Aloysius had been given all the little boys, and he among them, who had not yet made their first communion. At the House of St. Catherine they were instructed by the Priests of St. Charles in the mysteries of their faith. Their elder brothers were called the Church Boys of St. Lawrence, and when the great day of the feast arrived, they partook of the heavenly banquet, administered to them by the Holy Oblates in the Church of St. Mary's of the Angels.

Munday knew how the interior of the chapel would look, but now that he had reached the threshold of it he could not bring the sophisticate he had become to enter where the stainless child had once stood in awe. Here the voice of the Bishop had spoken out clearly to him, saying that it was St. Charles who prepared St. Aloysius for his first communion, and it was from the hand of the great Cardinal that the model and patron of youth first received the sacred flesh of his Divine Redeemer.

The place would be filled with miniature ships and numberless other offerings of the sailors who had been saved from death when the Virgin's glance had quieted the waters. But he could not bring himself to pass through the door. He turned away and saw his own footsteps imprinted on the sand below, the steps of a man who had walked with no agitation indicated in his gait to the granite steps carved in the rock. He walked back beside these prints, fleeing the chapel, but paying heed not to step where he had stepped before. But touch them he must, for they were the prints of a man who was himself, and he forced his feet into the fresh marks in the sand, seeking to efface them by grinding them into oblivion with his heels.

If he could believe again that in remorse there was redemption, then his own life might be saved for him, he thought. If he could feel remorse tearing and twisting in him, then his life might be redeemed. This was in his mind when he saw Ayton returning from the sight of the open water, his hair golden and his narrow, girl-like wrists hanging out from his jacket sleeves. The lift in his spirits when he saw the other man coming toward him told Munday he was not ready for repentance. Ayton was calling out words to him in an eager voice that shed their meaning before reaching Munday's ears.

At night they ate alone in the dining room of the hotel. The other tables were draped with clean white cloths, for it was not the tourist season. Lobster and snails in their shells had been served them, and a dish of Mère Poularde's omelette, as light as beaten cream. The tide would return by moonlight, Ayton said, and they lingered before the fire until it would be time to go out and wait on the wall for the sight of the water thundering in at three times the speed of a galloping horse, as the legend went.

Ayton was dressed in an admiral's deep blue, and whenever he moved in his chair a volley of shining arrows sprang from the fire to his glittering buttons and braid. Four gold stripes encircled each sleeve above the cuff, and his breast was strung with ribbons.

"A man should beware of what he eats," he was saying, preening himself like a vain woman. "Now lobsters and snails have the power to make a man grow a crust all over himself, and that's God's truth. I've seen it with my own eyes in countries where I've been. And, y'know, Munday," he went on with it, the "oye" and the "nye" of the cockney clanging softly on the air. "Y'know, in some parts of the world they won't let the young men eat venison because it would make them timid as deer. We may have shells like a couple of eggs by morning, after what we've eaten tonight." He sat talking and laughing and adjusting the cuffs of his handsomely decorated military jacket; and Munday listened, listened as if he could never hear enough of the voice or see enough of the little man sitting there. "To eat lion's flesh will make a coward brave," Ayton was saying. "They never gave tiger-meat to the women, the savages didn't, for fear it would make them too strong-minded." He sat still a moment, looking straight into the fire. Then he said: "I've seen so many people in my life, it's a good thing to see great, silent stones that never speak. I didn't go down to the *bistro* for a week, not even to look at the harbor."

"Not even the day your ship went out?" asked Munday, but his heart was at peace.

"Ah, don't now," Ayton said, and he lifted his hand as if to ward off a blow. "I couldn't have the both of you, could I? I had to make the choice."

It might have been that the young boy of other years had sat and talked with the Bishop close to the mouth of this same chimney, for Munday remembered that they as well had stayed late by the fire, waiting for the tide to turn. Once back in England, he had sat at his student desk, writing: "When I lay down I soon dropped off into a deep and refreshing sleep, and did not wake again until the moon was shining on my pillow. I stole out of bed to the window, and it was a lovely sight that met my eyes—the breakers gamboling and leaping upon each other's snowy shoulders in their wild race to land."

"Brandy must be a decoction of hearts and tongues," Ayton was saying. "For when I have drunk it I fear nothing and talk becomes the easiest thing in the world."

Munday knew that after a little they would get up and climb the open, spiral stairway. The bedroom door would close behind them and there they would stand, curiously altered, as if they had hung their own beings like cloaks outside the door. The two men who had climbed this high together would suddenly come face to face and whisper each others' names, and lie down on the bed together. And the tide would come and the tide run out again, for all they would know of its coming or going.

CHAPTER XII

IN the morning a masked sun hung over the Mont. Everywhere where there had been before a continent of sand, there was now the sea, and a new world come to life upon it. Fishing boats were setting out in coveys on the swelling water, and sardine boats rocked like cradles, with their nets hanging from the masts. All about the island's wall lapped the deep, strong, newly-risen sea.

Through the fieldglass' solitary eye Ayton could make out of the faces of the fishermen in their dories, as intimately seen as the lines in his own hand. He could not stand still for wonder and delight, and in his elegant clothes he stepped a dance before the telescope's brass legs.

"Ah, Munday, look!" he cried out. A sheep was grazing along the marshlands with no concern for the audience that saw it framed in glass. "Two miles away!" cried Ayton. "Two miles away, and I can count the curls on its forehead!"

The town was mute except for their voices sounding out against the stone. The granite itself made a deep well of silence in which they dropped their words and waited for the echo to return.

"In the summer it's bedlam here," said Munday. "Given over to the English with a vengeance, in spite of the monks having withstood them through the Hundred Years War."

"And now we share it with the beggars," said Ayton, for

there were bundles of rag squatting, like sick hens hunched in their feathers, in the cold, unaltering shadows. Ayton sat down beside Munday at the table on the terrace and asked, "Which holy man was it who said that the poor are always with you?"

"It was the Lord," said Munday, seeking now to speak of such things merely as history, saying "the Lord" without light or doom in his voice, as he might have said "Bonaparte" or "Disraeli." "It was the Lord when he sat down to supper with Lazarus."

"What way do you think of it?" asked Ayton. "Do you think it was so, Munday, that the Lord brought Lazarus back from the dead, or do you think it was that he gave the man a new reason for living? Through love," he said, hesitating over the word. "Do you think through love he gave the man a new taste for life?"

A damp wind had sprung up across the waters, drawing the clouds like veils over the figure of St. Michael. He stood in stern perfection, high on the tower that was greening with weather, war-like and exalted in his strength. Munday looked up to the sight of him, a bronze keel riding the drifting spew of cloud.

"I believe that he brought a man back from the dead," said Munday. He had believed it for so long that he had no thought of questioning it now. New truths he would have, but the things that had lain a long time within him must wither slowly from the stalk. "I believe that," he said.

"Ah, well," said Ayton, sitting humble and diffident in his chair, "how I look at it wouldn't have any point to it. It would only seem an uncanny thing to you to think you were sitting here with a man resurrected. I was as good as a man a long time dead," he said, his eyes fixed on Munday's face. "I'm sure they were looking me over, trying to decide if Hell was too good for me when you took pity on me. You started everything over again for me, like putting the sight back into my eyes when I never thought I'd like looking so much at anyone's face again, and putting fresh air back into my lungs."

Whenever he spoke in this way, the words touched the facets of Munday's being. The vulgar "oi" and "ing," the restless eye gave to their kinship its exact import; he knew he could be won, over and over, until there was no end to it, won by the weathered skin below the ear, and by the gold cap on the little man's tooth that shone in one corner of his mouth, by the wrists hanging out of the military jacket's sleeves and the color rising in his neck as if in shame.

"Then perhaps I've only done you harm," said Munday. "The Lord said as well that any man who loved his life should lose it."

"I say, that's evil teaching then," Ayton said.

He sat tapping his foot on the stone floor of the terrace and looking out to sea. This he would have none of, ah, none, ah, no! It tasted too bad to him. God could not have his vengeance every way.

"Why do you give me nothing but bits of your mind, Ayton?" asked Munday. "It might be a string of beads, broken and scattered, lost here and there in corners."

"Are you passing judgment on me?" said Ayton softly, and he looked down at his child-like hands. "You're thinking, you mean, of the string of pearls I found diving?"

"No," said Munday. He was thinking that if you drew the truth little by little from a man there might be some kind of salvation for him. "I was thinking of things that have been clearly spoken," he said, "such as the words of Christ, which in the Church are taken without question. But once out of it, then I can appease my own appetite for knowledge. Out of it now," he said, "I shall begin, late as it may seem, to feel myself more guilty of a deed than any man who has ever sinned, or at least as guilty."

Munday heard his own voice holding forth, and the escape, he thought suddenly, such as he had believed he had made from the accumulation of his youth, was only a delusion. The Church had not been set behind him, but was present in his marrow; he had never rebelled in spirit as long as the curious manner of speech and the spiritual, manly mating of the Church was there. For all his love of the Virgin's face, he had not turned to woman, but to man.

"All men must guide their life toward some image," he went on with it, "and mine is music. I do not believe any more that the Church of Christ is for all men. It was made for the fisherman and the ignorant who have no other vision, such as the humble men of Galilee." He heard his own voice speaking as if it was that of a stranger speaking. He might have been sitting at the table on this chill day listening to two men within him exchanging words he was not familiar with. "Music is mine," he said, as though this would save him. "I do not believe, not any more, that a man who loves his life must lose it, for if you can love one thing better than your life, then you are saved." And now he was becoming impatient. "Saved?" he repeated, mocking the stranger who sat there preaching to them. "Very well, saved for your own conceit, which is the opposite of all Christ's teachings."

"Having been a long time dead," said Ayton softly, "this is a strange language to me."

"You yourself taught me a new one," Munday said, "on your return from the dead."

"But one I learned right enough from the living," said Ayton softly.

The church itself that soared above them could not be visited unaccompanied for fear of what the ignorant might destroy, whether its silence or its vulnerable beauty that had endured. So a guide must herd all visitors through the labyrinth of stone. But the two men tarried behind the few others, lingering in the nave, and in the prisoners' pits. Pilasters, frosted over with design and color stood in the chapels; and on one of them Adam and Eve, with dismayed faces, took flight from the implication of God's finger. Out, out, out into the beyond, God was pointing, out and away!

"God, y'see, they say is Love," whispered Ayton. "And that is what Love does, y'see. It binds the two of you together, hand and foot, and then it sends you out alone."

They followed the others through the greenish chantries, linked arm-in-arm as Anglo-Saxon men were loath to do. Men walked so in foreign cities, in the streets of Genoa, without insinuation, or youths walked so on college lawns before they had grown to leave poetry and all the fairest things far behind. But now the guide missed them from the party and returned to seek them out. He nodded curtly to the Trinity' as he passed the altar and came toward them, suggesting with his keys that they follow the others into the cloister.

"Even here," said Ayton, "even here they're after us."

"Your hand is cold," said Munday. It's not the time of year to dress in white."

"I may never have the chance again," Ayton said humbly.

He held close to Munday's arm as they went out the wide door and into the garden of low, embroidered arches; and although they had stepped outside, the sky was not visible to them because of the stone that soared above their heads. Munday could see them as they must be, two young men walking side by side into the cloister that he had thought to know so well; but what had he known of it except its surface until he had listened to the two men within him talking: here had the zealots of the Congregation of St. Maur lifted up their homespun hems and climbed into their little basins, gossiping among themselves, or else telling their chaplets, while their feet soaked clean below them. Each monk had possessed his own trough, and in the more lavish ones, visiting Cardinals and Archbishops had paddled. The granite basins into which

95

these dignitaries had climbed for their ablutions were like drinking fountains set low around the walls.

A man asleep might have lain so and seen the two young men come clearly through his dream, speaking and loitering and pointing out to each other each stone flower. They were strangers to him, both, thought Munday, for all his heart was moved by them. He watched them in his mind's eye crossing the flagstones where pilgrims from Ireland and Italy had, six centuries earlier, set their sore extremities at rest. If he could lie quiet, asleep for a while, he thought, he would come to know the two men, and each would solve the problems of the other and give him an unmistakable face.

It was the light-eyed naval man, with his visor cocked who walked with him, who stooped now to examine the ornate stone fringe that hung as delicate as lace beneath the basins. The guide had moved on again with the others and was pointing out to the group the lofty court beyond the cloister which had once been the ecclesiastical garden, but which was barren now. By the column's base stood a mason's hammer and pail, and the other stranger was standing beyond it, paused dark and inward with thought, but smiling, like a man listening to good music being played. That would be Munday, he thought; that would be Munday waiting to be revealed to himself.

It was the naval man who looked up swiftly and said: "I say. I'd like to have a piece of that carving."

He reached his hand out for the hammer by the column, lifted his head quickly to eye the guide then struck the fine edge of carving a sharp and certain blow. What morsels of chiseled lace cracked off and fell he scooped up in his two bare hands and thrust them inside his fine jacket.

"Lucky!" he breathed. Then he dusted off his hands, settled the brass buttons and decorations on his chest, and stood again by Munday's side. "Whack!" he said. "Pretty nifty. Like killing a rabbit with one swipe of the hand!"

96

CHAPTER XIII

I N another week a miracle happened: it was the beginning of February only, but suddenly the whole world
blossomed into spring. In the fields near Cancale-Ville
there were now little goats, fresh as dew, sneezing at the
teats under their mothers' bellies. They had come into being overnight, but already they were chasing the goat-
mothers across the grass. Up went their stiff, uncertain
forelegs, straight and white, and out behind went their
hind legs, fluttering like bonnet-strings on the air.

But in a week the two men came back again to the city.
On the cliffs there had been some spice in the weather, but
here in the dark town it was raining foul, deathly sheets
of rain. They were back, and Ayton came into the room
and bolted the climate outside the door. But it was there
on the skylight, tapping for entry.

"I'll have the fire going in a minute to dry us out," said
Ayton.

He took off his officer's coat and set to lighting the fire
while Munday filled up the saucepan for tea. In the box
by the door were three letters: one for Munday, Edith's
scrawl over the envelope for Ayton, and on the back of
a menu the Alsatian girls had written:

"The *bistro* is no place for you. The sea came up so high,
it came right into the cafe. We'll come in any day you want
and see you at home."

Whichever way he turned his head, Munday knew the piano was standing mute in the corner. He put the water on the coals, and a great elation filled his heart. If he turned to it, he thought he would run to embrace it, for he could not walk soberly to it. But when he did turn, its dignity startled him. It was waiting, but with no need for preparation, like the strongest and purest souls are prepared for gentleness at any hour of day. He walked across the room to it and touched its face, and a shiver of pride ran through him. I have had a time of rest now, he said in his heart, and now I shall give my life a meaning. He laid his fingers on the keys, and one by one the deep syllables spoke out across the room: *Ego te absolvo!*

The sound of it had scarcely ceased when he thought perhaps it was in this way that Ayton's blood rose, clear and perilous, for a ship's prow and the things it could bear him to. The little man stood near the stove, reading his letter from Edith, page after page of it, slowly, slowly reading and sipping his cup of tea. In a while he put down the letter, folded over, and stood buttoning his black seaman's shirt at the neck.

"Drink your tea, Munday," he said. "It picks you up wonderfully, you know."

But Munday had ripped open the envelope in his hand and now he tossed the check out to Ayton.

"Well, our money's come," he said.

"It comes that way every month?" asked Ayton, picking up the paper. "Ooh, jolly! Nine pounds. That bucks a man. Nice to have your people, isn't it, standing to in the offing."

"Yes," said Munday. "Old men in their graves who put their pennies aside for what they wanted me to be. We might go out," he said, "and have a drink and something to eat in the *bistro*."

"You go," said Ayton shortly. "I'll stay home and drink my tea."

But still he went. He suddenly sprang to life and pulled on his tweed jacket. He combed back his hair, tight, thick, clotting the comb.

" 'Now in these days of indigestion,' " he said skipping before the glass, " 'it is oftentimes a question.' What the hell," he said. "Part of the business. All a lark anyway."

"Tomorrow we'll face the future," said Munday, and they locked the door in the dark.

In the *bistro* were Blanca, Annchen and Sophia, the big girl playing the piano, with her strong tireless back swinging from side to side. Munday saw the two girls, and the others in the cafe, alive with speech and action, and smoke hanging motionless on the air.

"*Aber*," said Blanca, swinging around on the stool. "You didn't get my message in the box?"

"Ah, yes," said Ayton, and he took the talk to weather and wind, and really had the sea come into the *bistro* that week, and Annchen leaped to her feet crying wildly "*la mer, la mer*" as if it were then, at that moment, about to rise upon them. She seized Ayton's hand and drew him out through the people to show him the water mark left on the outer wall.

Blanca sat there alone, a cigarette held in her hand, and Munday standing beside her.

"You're a fool not to be keeping Ayton out of sight," she said to him, her voice lowered. "They've been after him for a week now. The harbor police have been in here every night, and a couple of dicks who know him, having a look around."

"I don't know what you're talking about," Munday said, his eyes on her flawless, alabaster face.

"*Aber Gott*," she said quietly. "Didn't you take him out of town on purpose?"

"No," said Munday. He was fixed there, as if under a charm, feeling nothing, seeing nothing but her impassive face.

"But you knew Ayton deserted?" asked Blanca.

"No," said Munday. "We went off for a trip together."

"Oh, well, then," said Blanca, watching the smoke drift from the cigarette in her hand. "Well, there've been some things stolen. You'd better take care of him, Munday. They're after him with a vengeance because of his *dossier*."

There in the *bistro*, in the smoke and the heat, a fury seized Munday. He put one finger inside his collar as though to loosen it, before the outrage that bubbled like a hemorrhage in his throat would be the end of him if he did not get a blast of air. A righteous wrath was storming within him, tossing his thoughts this way and that like ships at the mercy of a thundering sea.

Ayton the thief, the thief Ayton, were the words that kept surfacing from the tumult, Ayton the little ape, thieving and chattering and wheedling, with his fingers running thither and yon the way mercury runs, Ayton the messenger of the gods and of eloquence and travel, Ayton with the first mate's and the commander-in-chief's decorations and buttons and braid on him aping the status of other men, Ayton who knew nothing about music, parroting the measures that other men had given their hearts and souls to, century after century, Ayton who had shattered the stone lace from *Le Merveille*.

Ayton was dancing now in another man's arms, and Munday made his way through the tables, and on the dance floor he shouldered aside the other dancers. Then he laid his hand on Ayton's shoulder. "Come along," he said quietly. "We're leaving now." For a moment, it seemed to Munday that the jangling music had been brought to a stop when Ayton freed himself from the other man's arms.

"Going?" he asked, and the music went on playing. "But we've only just arrived."

Munday jerked him sharply around and their faces came so close that they might have embraced each other. Out of the circle of faces he hustled Ayton, and the words that had been on the little man's tongue were left hanging behind on the air. Into the dark, dripping evening Munday bounced him, step by step, down the long, deserted quay.

Ayton tried to brace his feet against the cobbles, but the pace Munday had set never slackened. Ayton's hands tore like a child's at Munday's hand, but there was no relaxing of the righteous, iron grip.

"It isn't fair!" he cried out. "It isn't fair," his voice raised like a child's voice in complaint. But when the little jet of his irritation died in Munday's silence, he did not plead again but turned to other ways and means. "Ah, Munday," he asked. "What are you going to do with me?" he asked.

The quays were dark and still. Rain was beginning to fall, and the ships standing close to the stone were as massive as prisons. Between the wall of the ships and the bleak warehouses, the two men hastened down the narrow corridor of the quay.

"I'm afraid," said Ayton softly. "I'm afraid. Where are you taking me? What will you do?"

"I'm taking you back to your sister," said Munday, almost savagely. "That's what I'm doing. I'll tell her what you've got into now and she'll have to get you out."

But even as he spoke, his ears were waiting for the words of Ayton's protest. Suddenly his anger rose again and he shook the little man fiercely.

"Ah, you're hurting me," said Ayton. "You're hurting my arm."

"You're going back to your sister," said Munday. "She can get you out of your trouble. Don't say a word to me!"

"I'm not," said Ayton softly and obediently from the darkness, but Munday did not relinquish his hold on him.

"It's no good protesting," said Munday, "for I won't pay any heed to you. I'm through, once and forever. There's nothing more to be said."

The night was dripping all about them, and Ayton stood small and wet in the barely falling rain, his head turned away from Munday, giving no sign, making no sound. In the basin, the wild seawater was quietly coiled in sleep, or calm as if oil had been poured on it. Even the past, thought Munday, might be snuffed out forever by the rain and the darkness, and he would be a free man again. "Don't speak!" he cried out. But then he could bear it no longer. "Well, then, speak if you will," he said. "Let me hear what you have to say."

"Edith's gone back to England," said Ayton softly. "I've had a letter from her."

"Then you will join her in England," Munday said.

"The first places they'll watch is the ports," said Ayton humbly. "If I go near a crossing, they'll have me right away. I never wanted to deceive you, Munday," he went on saying. "I never had anyone, never, who thought me a grand man at all. I wanted you to believe in me. I wanted you to more than anything else in the world," he said, and his voice seemed to break in two with grief. "I wanted to make something worthy of myself after the years of it being the other way 'round. I thought the uniforms would please you. I thought it a fair enough way to start off the beginning of our life together, instead of coming to you like a pauper. I don't own anything like other people do," he said. "If you don't want me, I'll go away of myself. I'd be the last one to bring any disgrace on you, but there's nothing criminal, Munday, in the things I've done. I just had bad luck, it so happened. If I stay quiet a while somewhere, the trouble will blow over."

"The trouble!" said Munday. It was the first time the thought of it had come into his head. "The trouble may blow over soon enough, but that's not what I'm thinking of!"

"Ah, don't cast me off," said Ayton, and again his voice broke. "Something terrible may become of me if I have to be without you."

"You took care of yourself well enough in other years without me," Munday said.

But now another voice began asking questions of him, asking if for the filching of a few brass medals, and a handful of decorations for valor that he had no claim to, and the elaborate buttons befitting an officer on a jacket that wasn't his, were enough to send Ayton off to perdition? *Hush, hush,* said the black lips of the night. *If you have a child in your heart would you abandon him? Be still, be still. If anything like love has come to you, would you drive it out into the cold? Don't pass judgment on him, don't condemn him out-of-hand,* said the voice, like that of a mother giving counsel to a son. Then suddenly the harbor was slapped against the quay.

"Must be a boat passing," Ayton whispered.

Munday looked toward the harbor. "No lights," he said.

"That's just why," said Ayton, and he turned his head warily, as if to smell out some warning on the wind. But his hand had dropped on Munday's in caution as a blind shaft of light flashed across them from the water, hesitated an instant before passing, and then returned along the quay-side, as though seeking the sight of them again. Ayton skipped behind a fishing-dory turned bottom up to drain, and Munday followed him, and there they crouched while the funnel of light moved slowly, with precision, over the wharfs and the blank facades of the warehouses, casting a moment's illumination on every stone and pane.

"They're on the lookout for what they can pick up," Ayton whispered, holding himself clenched to keep his bones from shaking apart.

"You're cold," Munday said, and in the cramped place he took off his wool jacket and put it around the little man's shoulders.

"But what about you?" Ayton asked. "There's room for the two of us under." He laid the half of the coat around

Munday, and his hand lay cold and still on Munday's hand. "I'd hate to go to prison again," he said.

"We'd better try and make for the country," whispered Munday after a little. "If anything separates us, just keep on going on the road out over the marshes, to the quarry."

The searchlight was moving across stone after stone on the quays beyond them.

"But we won't get separated, will we?" said Ayton, his breath shaking through his teeth.

CHAPTER XIV

THE rain no longer drenched the earth but was a sly
affair lurking in the grasses and bushes as they
walked. They had come through the village, and now it
hung behind them like a mirage in the mist, falling into
rot and corruption on the bogs that sucked the life itself
from the foundations of the ancient houses. The two men
went along the road that led to the quarry, with the universe turning from winter in dissolution about them, dripping silently from the cliffs, and the rocks, and the
branches of trees they passed.

It was the end of the night, the first slow breaths of it
revealing the shape of walls and treetops. Far, far away
above the dark mass of the sea, the sky was turning pale,
fading slowly to a cave of light. It was just before dawn
when they came in sight of Quespelle's cabin.

Their footsteps on the path were a sign for the dog to
leap alive and swing at them in circles in the shadow of
the stone. A rock swelled there, offering no milk of kind-
ness to the shy sweet dawn, and in the shadow Quespelle's
cabin stood in foreboding with its sackcloth waving outward in the morning breeze.

A lantern shining behind the cabin opened a yellow par-
asol of light, and the sackcloth waving outward from the
doorway motioned away, away! Save yourselves now and
flee, go back, return to where you came from. Inside the

house a candle moved from place to place, seen first at a window and then in cracks of light between the planks, and the two men walked on with the shouts of the dog following them in warning.

Quespelle was coming from the shed, leading the horse's bony frame. The bridle was on the horse's head, and the bit ringing in his mouth, and its traces dragged in the muck behind. Once under the *ardoises*, Quespelle turned his head and peered through the lantern's light at them.

"Who's there?" he said.

They could see his dark jacket and the denim apron knotted on his belly. The black visor of his cap was pulled low over his eyes. Behind them lay the memory of the night's murmur and clamor, the sob of the boats on the canal in darkness, and the men with their searchlights on the quay.

"Are you off to Le Havre so early?" asked Munday.

Quespelle jerked his head at them and raised his arm to back the horse into the shafts of the loaded wagon. The mountain of vegetables on it could now be clearly seen, outlined against the sky. Quespelle gave them no word of greeting as he moved about the cart, groping with his thick, dark fingers, jerking the reins through the metal arch of the horse's collar.

"Pass me those baskets of potatoes," he said in a moment when the harnessing was done. He had no time for them; if they had no will to help him out, they should not be standing there. Already the rumble and drum of carts and hoofs could be heard on the highroad below. "It's not so early as all that," he said.

He lifted the baskets they carried to him, and in silence hoisted them beside the others. Along the road were the carts and burdens of earlier, brisker farm-men moving; his plants grew small, Munday remembered, as if for a dwarf's or a mean man's table; cauliflower as lean as a fist, potatoes in miniature riddled like a sponge.

106

It was not so early, but there was time. There was always time for coffee, and time for the cognac that brimmed up to the edge of the glass. For all of Quespelle's black taciturnity, there was time to bring the two visitors from the city in under the swinging cloth in the doorway.

"Leonie," said Quespelle. "Here are the two young men."

It might have been mid-day, so casually he spoke, and callers come at a reasonable hour. But his wife turned around from the heat of the stove and dropped the spoon she had been holding.

"My God," she said, and her hand fled up to her throat to fasten her blouse. "What brings you here at this time of day?"

Her hands ran over her thick, dark hair in consternation, mourning that they had come upon her so. When she turned back to the stove to lift the coffee-pot, Munday saw her young, grieving, suddenly turned beautiful face outlined against the fire's light. The two young men from the city, was her profile mourning, and me with a dirty old blouse on, and my feet out bare, and no patterns made in the sand yet. In a minute, thought Munday, she will fly off and put on black kid gloves and a feather boa for us, and then everything will be alright.

"We're running away from the police," he said, and he could not take his eyes from her face.

"It's all such a rum do," said Ayton, stretching his hands out to the heart of warmth in the cabin while Quespelle poured out three glasses of cognac and drank down his own. Leonie said not a word but set the coffee pot on the table. Then she looked eagerly into their faces.

"Well, if they came here," she said, "they wouldn't find it so easy. They'd just as soon pick a man up for one thing as another. The keeper of the fields came here once asking for a dog license, and for a passport, and for this and that. And he came only once, I can tell you. We haven't time for the police here. We're too busy," she said. "They never can tell you what it is they want to arrest you for. Just because they don't like a person's face. Oh, yes, sometimes it's nothing more than that." She tipped up the coffee pot and the liquid ran out like a narrow black ribbon into their cups. Then she set down the butter before them, and bread, and their cups and saucers and spoons. "Accusing us of taking baskets from other people at market and branding our own initials on them, or anything that happens to come into their heads," she said. "You have to have so much patience with the police. If you have enough, you can get the best of them. If you just sit still wherever you are, they can't do much.

They sat down to drink their coffee, and the fierce climate of the kitchen stove was scorching the flesh from their bones. The long hours of the night had made them famished men, the two of them outlaws and petty thieves, thought Munday, and he passed his hand over his face. In his palm he could feel the strong hairs of his beard beginning to push for life beneath the skin of his jaw.

"They're all against Quespelle," Leonie went on with it, "because he hasn't a regular hired man to help him. The police are all for the big farmers, and Quespelle's no good to them because he has only one cart and horse instead of a string of them, and no regular man to help him out, only Martin, the *gosse* who comes in from the neighbors."

Quespelle drank down another cognac and tipped his visor over his eyes, content that the conversation had turned to him.

"How would you like me for a hired man?" Ayton asked, and he smiled into the Frenchman's dark, brooding face.

The smile was so young, the eyes so filled with vulnerable, shy light, that Munday lifted his hand as if to protect Ayton from whatever might next be said.

108

"You'd have to grow a beard for disguise," he said, thinking he would do the same.

From the sudden realization that the room was swinging, he knew that he had drunk the cognac too quickly in the heat. Honor had perished, the statue he had modeled for his life was falling piece by shattered piece into obliteration, as the rain was falling drop by drop on the tin roof overhead. In his days and nights with Ayton there was a flame approaching the fire that leaps at the earth's heart, he thought, and for this he could put his music for the time aside, parked in the vestry until a better day dawned. They would survive landscapes scaled down to a mole's track, bubbles of earth that worms, like entrails disemboweled, gasped out seeking the light of day. He would skulk with Ayton in this twilit and alien country for a while.

And then what will we do, he asked himself, and the only answer that came to mind was that after the drama of flight was played out they could put their coats on and be gentlemen again. Everything he owned could be sold for a price, and the proceeds take them on foot to another country.

"I wonder how much I could get for my piano?" he asked of Ayton in his madness.

"You must be out of your mind!" cried Ayton. "Are you heaping coals of fire on my head?"

The Cockney turn of the little man's voice, the wain and the wan of a man from another place entirely might have been anything: a locust flying, a grasshopper cracking up his hindlegs like a jack-knife to sprint through the savage jungle scene in the heat of the room. *A thicker skin you'll have to grow*, Munday admonished himself, *and cultivate a wider vision*, in ridicule of himself doing nothing but playing a piano's keys.

After Ayton had spoken, Quespelle took another glass of cognac, and turned the idea over and over in his head. With someone to help him on his land, there might be no end now to the extent of his possessions. They would work their way in time to the very edge of the canal, into the rich flourishing loam of the valley, filching and commanding, and even paying a little here and there if ever the necessity came. Acres and acres might they by persistence draw into their holding. Working in brotherhood against the keeper of the fields; against the Catholics; standing firm as outlaws against the wretched town itself, conniving whatsoever they could from the others in the marketplace in the early morning: baskets, cabbage-heads, or eggs fresher than their own.

"One of you had better climb up on the cart with me now," said Quespelle. "I need some help at the market."

Leonie walked out with them into the dawn. A canny white sky, an oyster-orchard of clouds and light, was arching out above their heads. Munday climbed up over the wheel of the cart and took his place beside Quespelle.

"You should have been off an hour ago," said Leonie in gentle rebuke. "You'll be later than ever and the prices all down." Quespelle took up the reins and slapped them on the horse's hide, and as the mud-clotted wheels turned, Leonie looked up at Munday, and he saw the concern in her eyes. "Monsieur," she said, "potatoes are thirty centimes a pound at the start, but bring them down to twenty if the others do."

CHAPTER XV

THE mornings that followed had several ways of declaration. It was not enough for the barnyard cocks to sing out their announcement of the dawn throughout the valley; it was, as well, the sneezing and snorting of horses passing on the road below when straws or pollen tickled their noses. The first moments of day brought such anxiety to the cattle, wherever they might be, that they lowered their heads and sobbed and moaned about its presence.

Munday could hear at night the roof above him sighing in the dark, like the creaking bough of a tree complaining. Then bit by bit, dawn after dawn, the damp boards of the floor came to light and the torn canvas of the mattress he slept on in this closet of a room. When he opened the unsteady door and walked into the wider area, he knew that the curved tin neck of the stove would be red with fire, for Leonie was up before any of the others had stirred.

She had no time for the dawn, and no patience with the evening when it began to fall. She had no forbearance for the season or the soil, no time to wait for things to sprout and grow. The presence of sleeping people might be lying behind the door: Ayton asleep in one bed and Quespelle in another, lying snoring, while Leonie would be down on her knees before the vines, looking deeply and scornfully upon them as if to shame them into flower.

"For the first time today it feels like spring," she said one morning, for in her impatience she was hurrying them through March into the temperance of April. "It isn't so bad here in fair weather," she said, as Munday followed her on under the *ardoises*. In her progress, she kicked the soiled, empty baskets aside this way and that. "It's hard enough on your friend," she said, "who's accustomed to nice things around him." She seated herself on a box by the barrow of potatoes and set to work rubbing their coats of dark soil away. She rubbed so savagely at them that the color came into her face, and out from her hands they flew one after another, white as wax, into the open bag. "You can see by his hands," said Leonie, "that he's not in the habit of working."

Munday looked down at his own hands with the bit of rag he was holding, working beside her, rubbing the potatoes clean. It was strange to sit so by a woman, listening to her voice speaking as he might have listened, without troubling to wonder, to one of his own kin. All things in women returned in spirit to the Virgin, but in the flesh to his mother, who had died young, for she was the only woman he knew. She might well have been the charioteer standing in command within him, holding the reins that ran gently through the flesh of any other woman who came near to him. He could not think when he had last sat so close, if ever, but he was at ease because of the work they had to do. There she sat facing him, pure and remote as a wedded woman always seemed to him; and there was her hand, like his mother's undaunted hand on cloth or food or needle, taking these things as deliverance, as if they could save her from despair.

"If it's a good day," he said, "then it's the time to start clearing the ground above on the hill."

"Your friend thought of that," said Leonie. She looked up at him. "It will be a good thing to see it put to some use."

"Ayton's gone over the whole land," said Munday as he worked. "He knows these things very well."

"He said the weather would break during the night and be fair this morning," Leonie said. "And that's what is happening."

"He's been waiting a week for the wind to change," Munday said.

"When I lived in Rouen," said Leonie abruptly, "I had nice things too. Maybe you wouldn't believe it?" She turned to him and smiled. "There's a square just in front of the cathedral where the tramways change tracks, and that's where my cousin's jewelry shop was then."

"My father used to take me to hear the organ in the cathedral," said Munday, tossing the potatoes into the open sack.

"No!" said Leonie in wonder.

"Yes. I wasn't ten years old," said Munday. It was there he had first heard the Mass in B Minor played.

"*Tiens!*" said Leonie, working again. "Maybe you noticed the jewelry shop across the street?" Munday shook his head. "Now it's moved to the port," said Leonie.

Here was his mother's same, eager turning to place and incident, to the numbers on doorways, or to the slightest altering of the look on another's face. But whatever Leonie said or however she polished the stripped potatoes clean, there was her life as sour as blackbread to her, he thought, as his mother's life had been. She had no use for the soil or the years spent on it, unless it might be how she could urge the vegetation into flower, or so it seemed to him. "Quespelle was a carpenter then," she said, "and, you know, being a carpenter did something very sensible to him. He used to work with wood and nails, walking in sawdust all day long, and smoothing the roughness out of planks. And at night he had plenty of time for the flute. If you're a musician," she said, and she glanced at Munday as if not quite certain of it, "you'll understand what it meant to him. But when he became a *wattman*, what happened to him was this. From seeing so many different kinds of people getting on his tramcar and getting off, talking and fighting, and riding home drunk at night, and people never having the right change, what did he do but get drunk to forget about them, and it made him queer in the head. After all his years of fighting in Morocco and being a brave man in one war or another," she said, and a veil of sorrow had fallen now across her eyes. "Some people should never be expected to work for others," she said. "It puts them in a position. Could you picture a carpenter hitting his wife?" she said in a minute. She shook her head and went on saying, "It wouldn't be the sort of thing you could imagine the father of *le petit Jesus* doing, but a *wattman*, you could easily think of a *wattman* taking a drink because he was tired, maybe, and slapping his wife in the face because he didn't like the look of her by the time he got home, and taking another drink to comfort himself for what he was doing, and hitting his wife again because she was crying, and taking another drink because he was sorry—"

"Yes," said Munday. "Even priests are given books on men and women so that they can understand these things."

"You yourself are Catholic?" asked Leonie, but she did not wait for the answer. "Yes, I can see it. Quespelle is Protestant, that's why he's so quiet. Only Catholics are used to talking and giving themselves away."

"Except the priests," said Munday. "They are the holy receptacle for other people's troubles."

"Well, the other men become strangers to themselves as well," she said. "In a little while a *wattman* can become a man who hits his wife when he comes home at night. And in another little while, he can become something else as well. Every night he has a little bag of money around his neck when he gets off the tram, and by this time he has forgotten what he was like when he was a young man, and can you imagine him taking the money from the *wattman's* sack and putting it in his own pocket?"

"Yes," said Munday, "I can imagine that too."

Leonie stood up and wiped her hands on her apron. A sun, like a light behind a screen, was flickering now on the eastern sea as she reached high above her head to the gray beams under the *ardoises* where bulbs of drying garlic hung. There she stood before Munday, her waist so supple and slim that it seemed almost pitifully vulnerable to him.

"How long have you been here?" he asked, and Leonie paused with the garlic bulbs held in her hands.

"Here?" she asked. "Two years. I used to work in my cousin's jewelry shop in Rouen." With swift, firm gestures she laid the garlic in the already over-burdened baskets, her fingers smoothing out their parchment tails and tucking them tenderly in. "Quespelle came in because the face of his watch was broken and he wanted a new glass put on it. He was a carpenter then," she said. She sat down facing Munday, and suddenly she began to laugh. "He gave me a shock!" she said. "I took up a pencil to write down his name and address, and when I said: 'How do you call yourself?' he answered, 'The slave of the fairest woman!' 'Where do you live?' I asked him, and he said: " 'For the moment I'm stopping at beauty's feet!' " Leonie's eyes were filled with light, and she kept on laughing like a schoolgirl. "His mustaches were longer then," she said, "and he looked quite a handsome man. So he told my cousin that he was a carpenter and if ever we wanted any work done he would make us interesting prices. So when we moved down to the port," she said, "we had him in to make the alterations."

She laid the white lengths of raffia around her neck, and from the woven tray of watercress on the table she took the green leaves, stem by stem, and lashed them into tidy bunches. These were the times and the talk, he thought, that her heart was sore for. Before they had come to the place, she must have sat silent, hour after hour, stripping the skins from potatoes or lashing the leaves of watercress into emerald bouquets. He knew well how his own mother had sat without speech at the window, with her thoughts knocking powerfully in silence in her head. No book, no needle-work, no edge of lace had ever rocked her despair to sleep for her. It was a male world of endeavor that had sent her son to England for his schooling and left her with her mouth shut tight in the company of father, husband, and brother.

"I'll tell you how it is," Leonie said, pulling the white ribbons of raffia out one by one as she talked. "If a man has all his wishes and hopes set on one thing, it changes his face entirely." She looked across the table at Munday, but absently as though she did not see him there at all. He might have been any woman in bonnet or shawl, or any priest opposite her in confessional; or so might the Virgin have spoken, having set her grief aside for a moment or two. "A son must be a great comfort," she said. "And Quespelle always wanted a son. Do you believe in God?" she asked without warning.

"No," said Munday, and he corded the top of the potato sack around as though he were wringing its neck. "No, I'm sure I do not. I'm sure I don't believe in God anymore."

"But how can that be?" cried Leonie.

"I believe in the idea of him," said Munday. "But I can see no reason for God himself now. He must have been a strong man at one time, but the Church took the wisdom and power of many strong men to give it one moral."

They sat quiet for a while, and then Leonie went on with the story she had been telling.

"Quespelle's never had anything he'd set his heart on, except for marrying me. The door-jambs he made were so crooked that you couldn't hinge a door on them, and in the end my cousin wouldn't pay him. So he said: 'If you'll marry me I'll become a *wattman*.' He was full of fine intentions. Love," she said softly, "changes the look of anyone. I believe in it, you know." She looked up from the scattered stems of watercress in her apron. "Now take your little friend," she said. "He must have a girl somewhere. You know how it is." Her hands lay idle in her lap for a moment, hands bitten deep with dirt and marred by use. But Munday saw the tips of her fingers curved inward as if on the strings of a violin, and as if in denial of any allegiance to the soil.

"You know how it is," she said. "Perhaps he is in love with one of those Alsatian girls who came out with you that first day?"

CHAPTER XVI

THE first thing that was there in the morning was an arm of a tree reaching across the soiled glass of the window. Munday lay a long time with his thoughts, harking to the whisper of Ayton's breathing and waiting for the arm of the tree to take shape from the fading shadows of the night. Quiet now, quiet, he said in silence to the sounds that began stirring in the cabin. Hush to the sound of Leonie rattling the coals in the fire. Like a child who has grown too fast, Ayton must sleep more hours than the others. Hush, you must let him be.

But no sooner had he put his foot on the floor than Ayton's voice spoke out.

"There's nothing on the earth to be said for the early hours of these cold mornings." said Ayton. "A bloke gets up and goes off like a char—"

He lay hugging himself in his own arms for warmth.

"Stay in bed then," said Munday as one by one he put on his cold garments.

"Is the weather good?" asked Ayton. Munday stood looking from the window and buckling his belt. The sky was dark still, but little pools of coldest yellow lay between the angry clouds.

"It's not raining yet," said Munday.

"Then I'll be up," Ayton said.

They drank down their coffee by the fire in the kitchen

stove, and then went out across the land. When Munday set foot on it, he felt the spring in the soil pulling at the soles of his feet as if reluctant to let him pass. It took them a long time to reach the top where the layer of earth lay in fresh disorder; there they picked up their tools and set in working where they had left off the day before.

Munday thrust his spade into the ground, and slowly turned the clots over; deep to the hilt it went with his foot pressing down on the rim, as Ayton had shown him. The earth was rich and full of promise, unused, virgin soil that, for all they knew, had never been sown before. But everything was halted in his body, as though a heavy hand had been laid upon him. The great weight of spring seemed to have fallen far and wide, and Munday found it difficult to make haste. Now and then he leaned over to cast the rocks aside, and then returned to endlessly turning the soil.

It was perhaps Ayton's strong, rhythmic action that made his own seem labored. The man moved from tree to tree, pursuing his work between two trunks and pitching out the clumps of earth, he and his spade seeming to devour the soil. The spread and grip of his legs, planted wide and balancing his weight, were braced for subduing whatever stood in the way. He was no ordinary workman preparing the soil for growth, but a master of all men and of all seasons of the year.

It was the supreme authority in Ayton's flesh that humbled Munday, this appalling, almost brutal power of his penetration into the land. Each thrust of the shovel gave increased fervor to his impassioned advance, and in the end he would have the whole universe, clump on clump, uprooted and turned to fallow land. He had no time for speech, no time to turn his head toward Munday. The urgency of every fiber of his being drove each thrust to the subduing of the earth, yet he was still not appeased when each attack was through. Now that it was spring, the wandering troupes had begun to come down the coast in their caravans, descending from the far north of the country as if the breaking of winter had set them free as well. Munday could see them driving down the high road past the quarry below, with hammocks of hay and fodder swaying under the beams of their wagons. He looked down from his work and saw them passing with their goods and live-stock. Their dogs were freckled like mulattoes and leaping in their coffeecolored hides in the impatience to be off and explore the town for what possibilities of garbage there might be. Arrogantly and forlornly, the caravans wound toward the village where they would stake out their tents, and tether their horses in the square. Quespelle had got sight or smell of the troupers passing, and now he came out of the cabin settling his good coat on his shoulders, and Munday watched him hastening down the hill.

"Not even a pail in his hand to bring back water," Ayton called out to Munday. "Look at the bastard."

Then he went back to his work, and Munday drove his own spade into the soil. He worked apart from Ayton, slowly beating the weeds down, hacking, destroying, clearing the impeding growth away. Here and there, when he stooped to cast out a stone, loose gobbets of earth pushed in under his nails. The ruthless action of the stamping out and the tossing away of all that was superfluous continued without respite, giving no quarter. Out, out, out with whatever interfered with the simplicity and power of the canticle that defined evil and good. Out, out, out, showing no pity, went his thoughts, keeping pace with the rhythm of his attack. Out, out, out, as he flung the roots of what was still alive to its certain death. And every time the sharp edge of the shovel cut deeply into the ground he could see the writhing earth-worms that it had cut in two, each half managing to go its separate way.

His thoughts were fixed now on death and destruction, whether of the weeds, or of his time in the Order, or of his music that had slipped into the past when he most needed it. But could it be, he asked himself, that the annihilation of a man, and all that he had been, might be seen as a preparation for his re-birth? Was not the crucifixion of Jesus Christ proof of the impotence of death, for had not Christ triumphed and would live for all eternity?

He told himself that he must now compose a musical prelude to death, a prelude in celebration of the death that seeks to destroy whatsoever stands in the way of man's long journey toward clarity. The score of it was beginning to come alive in him, note after note, bar after bar, crescendoing toward a thundering finale of brass and strings, while a tenor's solo voice declared that the death of one aspect of a man can be a beginning rather than an end. But Christ had been a man of virtue, not of sin, and what claim did he himself have to consecration, Munday demanded of his own pride as he struck savagely at the weeds. For there were evil men in this world, his mind went on with it, and he thought of the monk Rasputin, who embodied the flesh and bone and spirit of all that was hideous in the history of mankind.

The Russian priest could not be pardoned for any quality he possessed, for he had none; when the assassins struck him down, the evil power that lay within him coiled into itself more fiercely. The Savior had died in humility on the cross, and Munday cherished him for this; but at the moment, in the heat of the battle with the weeds, Rasputin was Munday's sole concern. He had seen him in nightmares all his life, standing before a fireplace in the reception room of the Czar's magnificent palace, holding in one hand an open prayer book, a holy book, and every now and then glancing up from the sacred page to consult the mirror above the fireplace, a mirror that reflected the closed door behind him. And when the threat of death became a reality, as the door eventually opened, officers of the guard burst in, ten or twelve strong.

Here came fine gentlemen in uniform, with black fur

muffs standing upright on their heads, gentlemen Rasputin knew well, calling out "Good evening," or some such greeting to him; and when he held out his hand as if in blessing, they emptied their revolvers in his body. But even then, prone on the carpeting, he was not an extinguished man. Cleanly wiped out he would not be. He would leave some kind of final stain behind. When the officers had got as far as the door, making their exit, he had raised himself on one elbow and shot one of the best of them, one of the youngest, dead on the threshold. Munday thought of Rasputin in his monk's skirts lying in agony on the rug when the officers of the guard leaped over their dead companion and ran back to bring the butts of their revolvers down on Rasputin's skull.

But even this was not the end, Munday remembered almost savagely as he worked on under the rising sun, the notes of the prelude dropping within him, one by one, as clear as crystal. He could hear the Russian officers returning by moonlight to see if Rasputin were really done. The wing of the palace in which he lay was dark, for no one had yet come in and found the body, and the water was slipping by, dark and quiet, past the grating of the porch outside. He could see them at the foot of the stairs: a group of strong, comely young men standing, hushed and uncertain, with nerves twitching in their cheeks and their high boots gleaming, as they looked uneasily up the curve of the stair.

After a moment they went up, walking on tip-toe, their own strength persuading them that Rasputin must now be dead. But he had brought himself to the edge of the stairs and there lay waiting for them. The Death, the Death! It rose in Munday like a thousand strings in triumph, the accumulation of it shaking his soul. Rasputin had drawn himself up on his knees to address the young men who came up in stealth through the darkness: "Murderers, traitors, gentlemen," he began. But they fell on him and ran their swords through him to the hilt. But even then, even when the strings cried out and the piano thundered in separate anguish, even then they had not subdued him. The moans of the wind were his life and his speech as they bore him down to the courtyard. The officers lifted him, raised him bleeding in his black skirts, a man still breathing, breathing; raised him high over the grating with his heart still faintly beating, and tossed him into the stagnant moat. And only then—ripple—ah, ripple—ah, ripple—ah, ripple—ah—growing wider and wider, growing until it touched the bank and the music was finally stilled.

It was the sight of Quespelle returning up the hill that interrupted Munday's thoughts. He looked up startled and saw the Frenchman coming toward him over the turned land. He carried in one hand programs of a theater company, and once before Munday he stopped and began reading the titles out to him:

"*La Legends de Geneviève de Brabant, St. Antoine et Son Cochon, et Le Soleil d'Austerlitz.*"

There was a smile of pleasure under his mustaches, and he balanced back and forth on his heels in grim satisfaction as he began to speak to Munday of the rise and fall of the French drama, its disintegration since Molière, the final collapse in the days of Jules Romains. Back and forth he balanced with the programs as he talked.

"*Le Soleil d'Austerlitz,*" he explained, "appeals to all Frenchmen, for the noteworthy points in Napoleon's life are like those in the life of any soldier. Particularly in the life of a soldier like myself who has done Colonial service and felt the knife of his country."

Proudly and bitterly he talked, as if he too had, like his Emperor, been exiled and rebuked by fate.

"It's the weakening of the Church's power that has taken the best life from the theater," said Munday, leaning on his spade and with his shirt sleeve wiping the sweat from his face.

"How's that, how's that?" Quespelle asked, smiling at such jargon.

"Molière, Corneille," said Munday as he held out the package of cigarettes to the Frenchman. "They were both of them Jesuit pupils. And Voltaire and Diderot were schooled in dramatic art in Jesuit colleges. It was the one center of fire and creativity, the Jesuit culture, and now that it's waned there's nothing to go on in its place."

"That's not the kind of argument that will convince a Frenchman and a Protestant," said Quespelle. He stood chewing in irritation on his cigarette, looking bitterly first at Munday and then at Ayton, as he worked within earshot down the side of land. Bitterly he sought some kind of retort, some sort of fault to find with the two of them. "It's a waste of time, what you're doing here," he said at last. "You'll never get anything to grow."

Ayton turned to look up at them, a light of health and vigor shining in his face.

"It's not bad soil, you know," he said to Quespelle. "I didn't expect anything so good. The stones just lie along the top, and the vines come out with patience. We have another week's work on it, I dare say."

"You'll never get anything to grow on it," said Quespelle. He stood smiling in self-approval and conceit at the little man below him on the hill. "The first good rain will carry your seeds down to the bottom. It's fools' work you've been doing all these days, but I thought you'd find it out for yourselves. Instead I have to tell you."

"Ah, but we're not going to plant on the slope!" cried Ayton, no shadow of rancor darkening his face, no muting of the eagerness of his voice. "We're leveling the ground off. We'll have six terraces, here and here, running between the stumps. There's plenty of rock in the quarry to make serve as walls."

"I suppose you'll hire a mason then to build them for you?" Quespelle mocked him.

"I've done mason work," said Ayton. "I'll take care of that myself."

"Oh, you will, will you?" jeered Quespelle. "Whose land do you think you're on?"

"Not yours. That's a sure thing," Ayton said, and the Frenchman stood silent, drawing on his cigarette.

"No," he said after a moment. "Perhaps not, but one day I might take it into my head to put you in your place."

"If it wasn't for your wife," said Ayton quietly, "We'd have moved on to another country. There's no other reason that's keeping us here," and he went back to his work.

CHAPTER XVII

LEONIE had little time to dress herself in her concern for making Ayton and Munday elegant. She gave them her little red comb for the beards that were feathering their chins, and after supper she sat them down before the stove and parted their locks this way and that and rubbed their scalps clean with Petrol Hahn poured into a little rag.

"I'll clean the shoes," said Atyon.

"Oh, no!" cried Leonie. A flower was blooming in either cheek, and she could not make haste enough for them as she ran from shelf to shelf of the cabin after a bit of soap and a file for their fingernails, preparing them for the play. Quespelle, the social outcast, stood trimming his mustaches as best he could at the piece of mirror she allowed him. "Don't take all the hot water," she said as he went to the table to wash, and whenever she looked at him her face went bitter as gall. "Other people want to be clean as well as yourself."

When he was done, he went out the door without a word, buttoning his coat with a singular pride in his own manliness, however shabby he might appear to be. Once he had gone, Ayton broke into song.

Munday stood in the doorway, looking out over the dark valley and harking to Ayton's voice singing about the road to Mandalay, where the flying fishes played, and the dawn coming up like thunder out of China across the bay.

It was all far, far in the distance, even the boats calling out in the night from wherever they happened to be. Distant, yet amazingly clear, he was thinking. At the same time far and yet close by, like the omnipresence of a planet. He could feel his own heart within his chest, its heart shape tangible enough to be taken in his fingers, as it had seemed to him when he was a youth. Standing in the doorway of the cabin, with the sackcloth pushed aside, he felt no need ever to move on to other places. He and his heart were at peace here, and there was no telling what the future might hold if any change were made. Everything should be halted and any misgivings silenced. Even the wind had ceased stirring, as if at his bidding, and the occasional lights below in the valley were motionless as candle flames in a quiet room. Here he and Ayton were held close, two tired men who, night after night, fell asleep after working the soil, as primitive man had done.

It was the sound of Leonie's voice calling out their names that drew Munday back into the cabin. There she stood, smiling, in the center of the room, with a long, yellow, tightly belted coat on, and on her head a dark red velvet hat, with a plume wound around its crown. She seemed laced and bound, her waist gone thin enough to snap in two, and the puffed shoulders of the coat accentuating her bosom, standing there decked out in clothes that grandmothers or great aunts must have cast aside. Around her neck was a fur piece of many little red-eyed rats that clung in desperation to one another's tails. She stood radiantly there before the two men, eager as a child, waiting to hear what the two men would have to say.

"Did you ever see such duds?" she asked them, laughing and pulling a pair of gloves over her fingers, short, yellow, cotton gloves with fringes shredding out at the wrists. Such a rarity it was to be going to a play that she seemed to be another woman there than they had known before.

"You look a wonder!" Ayton cried out.

Had Munday not at that moment seen them standing close to each other, it might not have occurred to him to compare them, one with the other, but here with the lamp light shining on them, Leonie was smiling into Ayton's eyes like a woman gone daft. Her breasts were pressing against the tightly buttoned bodice of the coat, straining with such fervor against the yellow cloth that it seemed to Munday that in another minute she might set them free. She might cast the coat aside, thought Munday, and seize Ayton in her arms and begin to dance. But what would Ayton do then, he asked himself, for the vigor of manhood appeared to have sapped entirely from the little man's flesh and left him wrapped in silence. He had put his hand back on the table behind him, leaning on it for support, actually wilting before their eyes.

Leonie looked from Ayton to Munday and laughed aloud in delight. And then she turned down the wick of the oil-lamp, and in the abrupt obscurity they went out the cabin door. It was dark, it was almost night, and the dog was slinking into his shelter, his tail between his legs; and before them, shafts propped up from the mud, waited the wagon that would go to Le Havre at dawn, after Munday had loaded it with the baskets of sickly, worm-riddled produce.

"You won't get much sleep tonight," Leonie said.

"I won't even try," said Munday. "After the play, I'll drive straight to Le Havre. I want to be there early." He put his hand under her arm to guide her from the muck of the descent, and the sleeve of the yellow coat, shaped by and warm with her flesh, lay gently in his hand. "I want to see the Alsatian girls—" Munday began, and Leonie took her arm away quickly.

"The Alsatian girls! Why do you want to see the Alsatian girls?" she asked.

"I want them to come out and see us," said Munday. He

could feel Ayton's presence behind them. "Ayton wants to see a few faces he knows."

"Oh, but you can't do that!" Leonie cried out. "If one person knows, then everyone will know! They might not tell it on purpose, but somehow it would come out. He's been so safe here," she said.

Between them they had taken all the joy from her; there was none of it left to bear into the players' tent. As they came down the road they could see the tent glowing like a bonfire in the center of the square. When they had come to it, Leonie sat down in silence on a bench under the canvas top amongst the crowd of country people, and the countrymen and the fine, sly actors on the stage all turned an eye on her, for she was not a part of the town to them, but a woman in a long yellow coat who was from a time and a place they had never known. She was heedless and blind to them all, and sat with her hands buttoned tight in her gloves, one folded over the other, her face set in something like despair.

On the boards, the professional lady had mistaken the advertisement for *femme-de-chambre* for something else entirely, and she was entering the old master's bedroom in a shiny blue silk chemise. She was getting right down to business, her legitimate business, there on the stage, perched on the side of the old gentleman's bed, and for the first time in twenty years it was made evident that he was beginning to feel the paralysis go from his organs and his limbs. Behind Munday stood Quespelle, laughing until the tears ran down his cheeks.

"O, Muguette!" sang the chorus of shabby female troupers. On their stiff bony legs they danced across the sharking platform. "O, Muguette, prend garde aux loup—oo—oo!" Without festivity they sang, and their knees knuckled out in their tights as they danced, no joy whatsoever in the spectacle of them, for the toil and privation of their lives was marked forever on their middle-aged bones and flesh.

The old man sat up in his bed on the stage and made passes at the lady in a blue silk shirt, in indication to the audience of his reviving youth and spirits. With faces in the audience distorted in hilarity, Munday felt the uneasiness of Leonie beside him. She sat watching the scene and shaking her head, turning to look at him every now and then in apology and shame, as if this were womanly dignity itself reviled, and she a party to the degradation.

"'Y a des loups, Muguette, 'y a des loups!" sang the women, and the patches and darns in their pink cotton tights rode up and down their legs as they danced.

Behind them, Quespelle's laughter rang aloud and Leonie turned her head in irritation. She raised her shoulders and shrugged the sound of it away. On the stage the doctor was dosing up the old bridegroom on his wedding-night, and the old man leaped about the boards in joy, shaking out the seat of his pants in his fingers in indication that his restored energy had already come to flower. In the tent, the men stamped with laughter, and Quespelle's voice fled up in high, unnatural screams of delight.

On the other side of Leonie sat Ayton, eating peanuts and laughing aloud, and Leonie looked away from him and shook her head. Munday watched her face, so close to his own, her lashes curling up, thick and dark, her silence rebuking the hilarity that rose to the canvas roof. The bold glances of the actors sidled to her every now and then as they played, but she gave no thought to them or to whatever their intentions might be. Instead, she must turn to Munday in appeal now that all she had been taught by virtuous women to believe special and pure was being defiled. In the semi-obscurity of the tent, he could see her face lifted to him, as if for unction, as the face of a postulant might have been, and he thought: This is the symbol and sign of temptation, but it was not temptation in the flesh, for his flesh was already given in love, although given in sin. He could accept and condone her grievous chiding of those who roared aloud their lust and exalt it to holy fervor; he could transform her condemnation to the wisdom of the Scriptures. Whether he believed the words now, or whether he had passed from the Church's belief forever, still he could speak to her in the unforgiving speech of the Prophets, as their voices spoke to him.

"Do you go to confession now?" he said to her suddenly, aware of the two-sided tongue in his mouth.

"Confession?" Leonie asked, and then her hand fled up to her face. "Oh, no, never now, never any more! What will become of me, Munday?"

"Nothing will become of you," said Munday, "Nothing harmful. Perhaps you will want to go to confession one day."

She looked up at him, determined now, unflinching and strong. I'll never go to the Church again," she said whispering the words. "It never showed me how to be patient and forbear. All my life I saw myself sitting still, in a big chair, maybe with a good husband on one side of me, and a child on my lap. But it was never given to me. Everything else was given to me, whether I asked for it or not, but that one thing I wanted was never given me."

"Maybe it will be given to you," said Munday, speaking softly in the darkness. "You are young, and things; come slowly in life, as if you grew slowly up to them. The Virgin," he said, "was not as young as you."

"'Y a des loups, Muguette,, sang the women, kicking their way across the stage, "'y a des loups!"

"But the Virgin was never a lost woman," said Leonie, whispering it to him. "I am a lost woman. I can't be saved."

She had come so close to him that her shoulder was touching his, but innocently, signifying nothing.

"How are you lost?" he asked.

"I don't want to be saved," she whispered to him. "Not from the thoughts I have all day in my head, and from the things I want, dresses and pretty shoes. I want them to be real. I don't want to be any more without them."

"What kind of thoughts?" asked Munday. He sat still, as a priest in the confessional might have sat, luring the shameful thoughts from her head. Her hand was in his and he could feel the soft cushions of her fingers. "Tell me," he said, "tell me."

"Thoughts," she said, and as she spoke, the breath from her mouth sighed across his face. "Possessing me. It's all Ayton. Ayton. It's the most terrible thing in my life."

I N the *entr'acte* the lights sprang up under the canvas and
the men, in a great stir of movement, wandered out
from the tent, putting matches to their pipes and to the
loose empty ends of their hand-rolled cigarettes. Even Ayton went out, lost carelessly amongst the others, with his
hat tossed aside on the bench where Munday sat.

"I want a drink," he said, and "Ah, don't be foolish now,"
said Leonie.

"I might as well be dead," said Ayton, "if I'm not to go
and come as I please."

Out he went, and Munday saw him bow down his head
and pass under the flap of canvas, and that was the last of
him for a little while. The leading man had now made his
appearance before the drawn curtains on the platform,
with a set of fine bright saucepans hanging around his
neck. There were rubies pierced in his ears and his white
Gypsy teeth were shining.

"*Ah, mes seigneurs, mes princes, mes princesses!*" he cried out
to them. "*Que la joie entre en vos coeurs! Regardez, admirez,
convoitez! Seul-le numéro gagnant emportera une série complète!*"

"Ah, the saucepans!" said Leonie softly, and she sat looking at them as if she could never see enough of their
polished faces. But when the acting-man began to speak
again, she turned to Munday. "When you're young," she
said, "you keep your thoughts to yourself because they're

too good to give away to everybody. I used to walk along the streets of Rouen thinking that. I remember very well how it was."

"Songez-donc, mes seigneurs, mes princes, mes princesses!" cried the actor from the stage. *"Vous n'avez pas encore ouie le grand Zizipanpan d'Amérique, pêché dans la Mer Caspiane à l'entrée du Golfe de Lion. Cet animal intelligent—"*

Munday looked down into Leonie's hands, young scarred hands with the nails worn off as black as elderberries. They lay still and heedless in her lap, and she spoke in a low voice to him.

"One day my father went off to pay a bill," she said, "with three hundred francs in his pocket, and he didn't come back all night. Whenever he would be away from our café for a time, Mama would always act very strange, sitting down and trying to talk with the customers that came in, or serving behind the bar, but with her talk entirely different from the way it usually was because of the trouble she was thinking he might be in. Mama walked up and down half that night," said Leonie. "I could see her. She was not angry, and she did not walk quickly, but instead very slowly up and down. She was faithful, as every wife should be."

The young troupers had begun to sell the lottery tickets throughout the audience, and now one stood before them, peeling the pink tickets off on his moistened thumb.

"Je disais donc que ce splendids animal que vous verrez tout à l'heure distribuera lui-même le premier lot!" the actor was saying as he leaned intimately toward the benches and closed one gleaming eye. *"Il mesure trois mètres cinquante de la tête à la queue et cing mètres de la queue à la tête, car ça va en remontant! Un peu de silence!"* he cried out above the men's laughter.

"It was the postcard I saw that afternoon I went out with Mama that made me remember it," Leonie said. "When Papa came home he hadn't paid the bill and he had no money left. It had been taken away from him by a woman.

He knew very well who the woman was but he wouldn't tell us her name." She sat talking to Munday, raising one hand and then the other, for these two had been witnesses, and she laid them on Munday's arm. "Mama took me by the hand, and the two of us, we set off to find the woman and ask her to give the money back. The policemen in Rouen and the tradespeople, and all the streetcarmen knew Papa's face and his business, and by asking here and there as we went along we found out little by little which way it was he had the habit of going. He was accustomed to going across the square and behind the cathedral, and then down the little streets that run off behind. That's where I saw the postcard in a window as we were passing. It was in the glass case of a paper shop, outside on the walk. It was the real photograph of a young man, with color painted on his cheeks, the kind of a card, you know, that has real hair on it, and he was holding a bunch of flowers in his arms."

The thought of it filled her with such pleasure that she began laughing, whispering and laughing softly in her tightly buttoned coat.

"*Y-a-t-il dans la société,*" cried out the actor on the platform, "*une personne chaste, innocent et pure—*" With this the men who had begun to return to their seats on the benches, with some bitter sort of deviltry in them, began calling out Quespelle's name. They brought him in through the opening in the tent, and pushed him toward the center of action, but he stood resisting, his short arms folded high on his chest and his mouth beneath his mustaches smiling grimly at their shouts of laughter. "*N'ayez pas peur, Mademoiselle,*" the actor cried, cajoling Quespelle in a high falsetto. At the sound of this the country people stormed anew. "*N'ayez pas peur,*" he cried shrilly. "*Mettez la main dans ce chapeau pour sortir le premier numéro! Ce chapeau,*" he told them in a high whisper, "*était autre fois un chapeau à Olive de Marseilles diont je vous raconterai l'histoire une autre fois.*"

Quespelle took a step forward and thrust his short-fingered, broad hand into the open hat.

"I wanted to stop there and have a good look at that postcard," Leonie was saying, the side of her face came closer to Munday's so that he might hear. "But Mama had this one idea in her head, poor Mama, she wanted to go on and find out who the woman was. So we stopped at the *bistro* on the corner, and they told us Papa often came there in the evening. 'Was his lady-friend with him last night?' Mama asked, as innocently as if she knew all about it. 'Yes,' said the *patron*, 'she was here crying like a *madeleine* because her boss had given her the gate.' 'So what will she do now?' asked Mama, as cool as you can imagine. The *bistro* man said he didn't know. 'I'd like to go and see her,' said Mama. 'Perhaps I could find a place for her.' I could see her looking slyly at the *patron*, but he had no way of knowing what it was she was trying to find out. 'You might very well run across her now at the *lavoire*,' he said. 'I know she was going there to wash her clothes before packing off.' This was a lot of help to poor Mama, for she didn't know what the woman looked like. Perhaps the boss was tired of seeing her step out so much in the evening?' said Mama. The *bistro* man put his elbows on the bar and leaned over toward Mama. 'Between you and me,' he said, 'it's the trouble she's got herself into. She's so big now you can see her coming a mile away.' 'My God, as quick as all that?' said Mama, and she sat down suddenly in a chair. 'Quick or not,' said the man, she won't get another amateur in a hurry.' Mama got up to pay the man for the little drink of syrup she had taken. 'So long as I have my little girl with me I won't go searching around the *lavoire*,' she said, 'I'll wait for her at her place until she comes in.' The man picked up the sous she left him as a *pour boire*, and she said 'It's just at the end of the street, isn't it?' as if she had forgotten. 'Not quite,' said the man.

'It's the house with the white arch just before you come to the corner.'"

"*Mes princes, mes princesses, mes seigneurs!*" urged the actor. "*Un peu de silence pour entendre la voix douce de Mogodor l'Androcèphale, géant qui fait avec sa queue ce que vous ne pouvez pas faire, mes seigneurs! Il a la peau des yeux tellement tendue que quand il ouvre la bouche il ferme le cue, quand il pet il fait du feu allumant touts becs de gaz de la mènagerie!*"

Here the acting-man broke down and cried out with laughter as well. He stamped his feet until the platform shuddered, and the rubies in his ears shone like drops of blood.

"I don't know what was going on in Mama's head," Leonie continued. "I was thinking of the young man I had seen on the postcard, and I was holding on to Mama's hand. We went to the strange house, and rang at the servants' entrance, and a *valet de chambre* with an orange and black vest on him came to the door. 'I wanted to see the *bonne*,' said Mama, smiling at him. Whenever she smiled at a man, poor Mama, she always got her way. 'She's up in her room changing her dress for the service,' said the *valet*. 'She's leaving the house tomorrow morning, the dirty slut.' 'She's a friend of mine,' said Mama proudly, 'don't speak ill of her.' 'Very well,' said the *valet*, 'you can go up this way.' He went to the foot of the backstairs with us and stood there looking up the backstairs after us until we turned the corner. Mama never wore a hat, but she had a scarf thrown over her hair. And she took it off when she knocked at the first door we saw before us. We waited there in the hall for a minute, for there didn't seem to be anyone in the room."

"*Mille cing cent quatre-vingt-onze!*" the actor cried out from the stage. He had lifted the winning number from Quespelle's fingers and held it up for them all to see. Leonie looked at the two pink tickets in her hand, and shook her head in disappointment.

"After a little while, Mama knocked again," she said. "And this time somebody on the other side of the door said 'Who's there?' The voice sounded very close to the door and as if the woman had been crying. 'I can't open just now,' she said, 'who is it that's there?' 'It's a mother and wife who want to see you,' said Mama proudly. 'You have to open the door to me.' The knob turned around, and the woman opened the door a little ways, and we could see her very well standing with her handkerchief up to her mouth and her eyes very red. 'I must speak to you for a minute,' said Mama, and she walked right past the woman straight into the room, with me holding on to her hand. In the middle of the room she stopped with me beside her, and the woman closed the door.

"She had no looks at all," said Leonie, "but she couldn't have been an old woman. 'Your little girl is very pretty,' was the first thing she said. 'You should have had a thought or two for her,' said Mama, 'before you made the *bombe* with my husband.' 'Your husband!' the woman cried out as if she was choking to death. But Mama was looking very sweetly at her. 'What do you want of my husband?' she said. 'Aren't there enough other men around good enough for you?' The woman stood shaking her head back and forth at Mama with her handkerchief up covering her mouth. 'You must know he's not a rich man,' said Mama, 'so why did you take the three hundred francs from him last night?' 'I can't give them back to you,' said the woman, 'if that's what you're after.' I can hear now the sound of her as if she was speaking out of a tight small hole. 'You probably, had your uses for it,' said Mama, without seeming to be angry. 'But will you, please, now that you see how it is, leave my husband alone hereafter?' 'I needed the money,' said the woman, 'to settle some debts I had.' 'God knows what kind of a creature you are,' said Mama, 'but if there's any good left in you you'll go about your business. I'll not say a word about the three hundred francs, but you must swear to leave my husband be.' Suddenly the woman began to laugh out loud, but the tears were running out of her eyes, and she took the handkerchief off her mouth to wipe them away. 'What have you done to your face?' Mama cried out when she saw it. The woman's mouth and chin were as red as fire. 'Oh, I'll leave your husband in peace, I promise you that!' said the woman. 'I drunk down that bottle of stuff there before you came in the door.' 'My God, there's still the time to save you then!' cried Mama, and she grabbed up the woman's hat off the bed and stuck it on her shaking head. I was holding on to Mama's dress and crying, but her thoughts were all for the poor woman, and she dragged her out the door and down the stairs. 'You should have thought first of your poor little baby inside you,' said Mama to her, and the woman started screaming out with laughter. 'My baby!' cried the woman. 'Ha, ha, my baby!' She laughed so loud that the *valet de chambre* came running up from the kitchen. 'You can't make a noise like that!' he said in terror of his skin. 'Oh, my baby!' shouted the woman. 'That's the funniest thing I ever heard!' 'The boss won't have it,' the *valet* said, and the woman started being sick all over the stairway. 'You can't do that,' said the *valet*. 'You're not allowed to be sick here.'"

"*En avant l'orchestre!*" cried out the leading actor from the platform. The violinist's head dropped on his fiddle, the flute began to pipe with wind, and the audience sought their places in confusion as the curtains parted before the dawn of the "*Soleil d'Austerlitz.*"

"We went all the way to the hospital with her," said Leonie, "but she died that night no matter what they could do."

Munday sat still beside Leonie, seeing that the story of death for sorrow, and death by poison had taken the youth from her face. Whether she remembered it all so, or whether her mother had told it to her, over and over again in the years that came after, still it was a grief to her and he must turn her thoughts another way.

"But you haven't told me," he said, "about the post-card . . . "

Behind them Quespelle was standing on a bench to see the stage better, and applauding with the others Napoléon's entrance on the boards. Leonie looked bitterly up at Munday, and after a moment returned from her mother's agitated life.

"Oh, yes, the postcard," she said softly. "I went back another day to the street where I had seen it and I bought the picture and I have kept it. I can show it to you in the cabin, for he was to be my husband. And do you know," she said, "it might be Ayton's picture—"

"Ayton," Munday murmured, and then he swung around on the bench. Quespelle, with tears on his face, was staring at the sight of Napoléon booted and spurred upon the quaking stage. "Have you seen Ayton?" Munday asked him.

But Quespelle stood motionless, with his tears falling: Napoléon, Napoléon, oblivious to any other name or to any other sound.

CHAPTER XIX

HERE the night was laid out as if with care between the troupers' tent and the trees, and when Munday walked out from under the canvas the air of it ran into his mouth and nostrils and swept the taste and smell of the players' fard and gunpowder away. There was a covered booth to one side, with a single light bulb shining feebly in the ceiling and a wooden counter running the length of the narrow space. And there with a drink on the counter in hand's reach stood Ayton, clean-looking and youthful in the dust of the square, Ayton speaking his mind out on one subject or another to the Gypsy barman on the other side. When Munday spoke Ayton's name, the little man turned around, his eye shriveled up as if he were facing a blazing light.

"I've been talking with a man named Rochereau, who was walking by," Ayton said. "So I know all about the political situation, local and nationally. I even had some solutions for him."

"Rochereau!" said Munday. But things had gone too far for him, and he could only stand and wonder.

"I told him about the holy nut of England," Ayton was saying, "vanquished by the drawers of water. Listen, there's one thing we have to do. I talked it over with the old bugger. There's no two ways about it. Have a *fine à l'eau*," he said.

A *gendarme* was pacing up and down in front of the troupers' tent, and Munday could not take his eyes from him.

"What is it you told Rochereau?" asked Munday, as he watched the *gendarme* turning back and forth between the stakes.

"We have to get those pipes and the opium out of Le Havre and try to sell them. I think we could pawn the medals. We have to get hold of some money," Ayton said, ignoring the question put to him. "We have to get away." He picked up the glass before him to set it in front of Munday, and the half of it spilled over and ran across his hand. "I told Rochereau about it. 'I wasn't made for truly rural scenes,' I told him. 'Now take Munday,' said I, 'he likes this part of the country. I like dramatic scenery myself, but Munday's quite satisfied where he is. Munday had a fine career in the city,' I said to him, and what did he do but give up the whole thing for a mess of pottage, as it were, retired, if you know what I mean, and come off to live quiet-like in the country.' 'I didn't know you were neighbors of mine,' said the old guy. 'Sure, we are!' said I. I told him where we were living. 'Right-o,' said the old bounder. 'I'll drop in on you one of these days.'"

The *gendarme* went back and forth under their noses. His hands clasped at his back and the heels of his boots sending up puffs of dust behind him as he walked.

"'My God,' I told Rochereau," said Ayton. "'My God,' I said. 'I haven't committed a murder after all. What have I done when you come right down to it? What I've done,' I told him, 'is something that happens in every port town every day of the year. Am I the first man with an officer's stripes on his sleeve to let his boat go off without him?' 'The hell you are,' said Rochereau."

"All right," said Munday, "but now we'd better be getting up the hill again."

He drank the *fine* quickly from the glass Ayton had set before him and took his money out.

"No," said Ayton in a grieved voice. "No, I can't. I can't go back to that place any more."

"Ayton, it's only for a little while," said Munday.

"That's what you say," said Ayton. "You keep saying week after week that it's only for a little while. I can't believe you any more. What is keeping us here, what are we waiting for in this foul part of the world?"

"We're waiting for the trouble to go by. We can save our money where we are, and when things are quiet again, then we can go off to another country," Munday answered. "When the time comes, we'll sell all our belongings, one after another, and we'll go off wherever it seems a likely place to be."

"Don't you ever feel the time has just about come?" asked Ayton, smiling into the glass the barman had set on the counter. "Munday, you must have another drink," he said, and he turned around and strangely enough reached out his hands to Munday. He might have been in a dark house alone, groping his way toward a strip of light showing under a closed door. "Munday," he said, "if I'd ever been to a school that taught me speech difficult enough to fit my thoughts, I could describe to you the commotion that's in me. When we've finished laying the new ground out, then let's be on our way."

Back he came to it time and again, back and back, like a fox flaring out the trail that would hush his steps behind him and save his elegant hide. Now the moon was up, and however the elements were his blood must rise with it, as if the bones of his body were secured in vengeance to the white spokes of a new moon that went climbing up the sky. "Forty years ago, I hunted ducks on this very block of ground, worth today a small fortune in itself. At that time there were only seventeen white persons in the town, and a tribe of Winnebago Indians encamped about three miles west of our village . . . "

"Yes, Ayton, yes," said Munday, speaking gently to him. He felt his own shoulders broad and strong in his coat, and he hoped they would block from Ayton the sight of the *gendarme* who had just walked into the place. "We'll walk home now," he said.

"Forty winters," said Ayton, and then he turned and raised his glass to the *gendarme*. "Forty winters have spread their white covering and as many beautiful springs have brought the birds and flowers to us, returning every season to a vastly larger population . . . "

The *gendarme* crossed over the stretch of boarding that lay between himself and the two men, and when he had come to where they were, he halted and raised his hand.

"*Anglais?*" he said.

"Yes," said Ayton. "There are fairies in the bottoms of our guardsmen."

"Will you have a drink, sir?" Munday hurriedly asked the *gendarme*.

"Good health generally prevailed," said Ayton. "There were no divorces, no aristocracy, no bankrupts, no deserters, no musicians, no envious heart-burnings because one woman had a flowered carpet in the parlor and another didn't have one. Ah, the women, they were indeed women in those days! To tell you the truth," he said softly, "I'm afraid of my life of the women—"

The *gendarme* jerked his head toward Ayton and smiled. He made a motion with his hand, and counted four, five, six times on his fingers, indicating Ayton had made away with one drink after another too many. Munday nodded and he and the *gendarme* stood smiling at each other over Ayton's head.

"Have you your papers, gentlemen?" he asked, and he took a swallow out of the glass before him and wiped his mustaches with the back of his hand.

144

"We just walked over from Le Havre," said Munday, feeling within the vest pocket of his coat for his papers.

When he turned his glance in despair to Ayton, he saw that something canny and clever was coming to life in the little man's face. He was looking slyly at Munday, his yellow brows beetling fiercely over his eyes. In the *gendarme's* pocket there must be lying his photograph and an endless tale about him, wanted for this, that, and the other thing, like any common thief. The *gendarme* had turned his mind to Munday's papers when Ayton again put out his youthful hand. *"Je vais rendre,"* he said, and he made a sour mouth at the *gendarme.* "I'm going to be sick as a dog in the gutter."

Munday watched him swaying down the length of the counter, moving away from them, his fingers skimming the side of the wood as he went. When he came to the end, his foot caught on the brace of the upright beam, and he hiccoughed as he turned the corner. Then he was gone.

The *gendarme* opened Munday's passport and held the French identity card in place with his thumb. From one page stared the smooth-fleshed face of a man who was filled with strife and passion and sorrow. Only in the benign mouth was there a hint of what the preacher in him might be.

"I've grown a beard since then," said Munday, touching his chin with the palm of his hand. The *gendarme* turned the identity card over and scrutinized the dates stamped on the back of it. When he returned it to him, Munday asked, "Have you seen the show inside?"

The *gendarme* picked up his glass and drank again, and a smile of pride transformed his face.

"I won the saucepans," he said.

As it happened, he started to tell Munday, it wasn't he himself who had bought the winning number. It came about in an extraordinary way. He had bought five tickets himself, and he took them out of his belt and showed them to Munday. All of them were far away from what the winning number turned out to be. But just as he was walking up and down in front of the entrance, he caught sight of a ticket that had fallen onto the ground. Nobody seemed to be looking for it, so what did he do but step forward and put his foot over it, deciding that if anyone came out and made as if trying to find something, he would turn it over to them as any honest man would do. But no one gave any sign of searching for it, so when the winning number was called out, there was the lucky ticket in his hand.

"But I don't call it luck," said the *gendarme* as he took another nip at his drink. "I call it destiny."

For a moment Munday almost smiled, and then he saw the figure of Ayton returning out of the darkness, coming toward them at a wandering, unsteady gait.

"I want to report a theft to you," he said, and he halted before the *gendarme*. *"Figurez-vous,"* he said, with a brooding, outraged lowering of his brows, "I had a lottery ticket. This was the number of it, marked down on the program: *Mille cing cent quatre-vingt-onze.* The very year that the French, bless them, gave Scotland and Wales back to the crown! Fortunately I wrote it down," he said, "for what do you think happened to my ticket?" Ayton ran his hand through the pocket of his coat and his fingers came out the other side. "It dropped out, as soon as I put it in, I suppose, right there before the entrance. Really, officer," he said, "there must be some kind of justice in the land."

"You can't be sure where you lost it," said the *gendarme* uneasily, and he cast an uncertain eye on Munday.

"Ah, yes, I'm sure," said Ayton grievously. "It was there, right there before the entrance. That's where I bought the ticket and put it into my pocket at once, but there was a hole in my pocket."

"Eh, bien!" said the Gendarme, and he looked again at Munday. But Munday could not speak in fear of what

question the *gendarme* might put to Ayton next. He stood silent, his eyes pressing more and more urgently on the *gendarme's* stricken face. *"Eh, bien',* said the *gendarme* again. "It's your good luck that it fell into the hands of an honest man."

"Oh, but a thing like that," said Ayton, "it's a matter for the law, you know. A man can't take another man's ticket that way. It amounts to theft, doesn't it, officer?" The *gendarme* finished his drink in silence, his face, with the stubble across the clefted chin, as tragic as any Munday had ever seen in church or funeral parlor.

"The saucepans," he said, and jerked his head over his shoulder. "They're over there."

"Was mine the winning number?" Ayton cried out. "Lucky for you," said the *gendarme,* "it fell into my hands."

In spite of himself he must turn to watch Ayton lift the stringer of shining pans from the shadow of the counter. "My God," said Ayton, and he threw the clattering array of them across his shoulder. "My God, what will Leonie say?"

"And what was his name?" asked the *gendarme,* his senses having come back to him now that Ayton had gone on his way.

"John Doe," said Munday, and he ordered another drink for the *gendarme.*

"Is he staying long in Le Havre?" the *gendarme* wanted to know.

"He's taking the midnight boat for Southampton," said Munday. "That's why he was off in such a hurry."

After the gendarme had finished his drink, he saluted Munday.

"Goodnight," he said.

"Goodnight, sir," said Munday.

CHAPTER XX

HOWEVER he thought of these things or others now, Munday must put them away to examine later. He must take them up onto the cart with him, ride down the hill and out onto the highroad, with Quespelle chewing tobacco beside him, and the reins lying across the dashboard and onto the horse's rump. The early morning was dark and cold, and the vegetables travelled in state like wilting queens behind them. The thoughts that ran with the wheels' complaint on the ruts went on despite him, and he planned to close his eyes to the sight of the sky carved out by dawn, and close his mouth to the fresh taste of morning, and think of nothing except the price of vegetables at the market.

He thought of the days that had gone by in the country, one by one, dwelling slowly on them, turning them in his mind as patiently as earth turned over. He thought of the side of the land, and the broken quarry, and even the little roots turned out, young and white at this season, and the seemingly dead and barren twigs of the rose-trees bound up by Ayton in strips of linen against the cold. Sitting so on the wagon he thought of the comforting fire of the stove in the room, and of the yellow sand strewn like meal on the floor; he remembered how the water sprang from the pump in the roadway, with icicles in its locks, and the sound of the timber of the cabin crying aloud as the wind passed through at night, remembering these things as if they were of the long ago past. It was the thought of Ayton now that drew Munday's arms up across his chest, as though he would warm them at the fire of his heart.

The road was leading out over the marshes, and the horse advanced slowly, slumbrously in its worn harness, the road-lights from time to time casting dimly shining circles on the rippling muscles of its loins. Then into the half darkness again they went until the next circle of light was cast down from above. Quespelle swayed in his seat, his visor lowered over his face, his breath snorting and blowing as if in sleep. Ayton must now be sleeping in the cabin, lying child-like and contented, dreaming of far countries, Munday thought, and poor Leonie, his mind went on with it, poor, poor Leonie, poor Leonie, poor child.

So it would be, he knew, wherever he traveled with Ayton. Wherever they went together, the heart of someone else must burn for love and yearning of what Ayton had to give. For the taste he had for life, everything else could be condoned. He was strong and willful and gleeful, thought Munday, the way everyone wanted a man to be. "Ah, come now," he could hear Ayton's voice saying: "If a bloke moves east like the stars and the tides do, Munday, there's no harm in anything at all." Wherever they moved on to together, then somebody else would be stricken, wanting a year, of a lifetime, or something else of Ayton. Poor Leonie, he thought, poor Leonie; and in another little while it might be poor somebody else again.

Surely the broad, rump of the snoring man rocking beside him on the wagon, with the charred remains of a cigarette hanging now from his lip, must make his wife's blood curdle in her veins. And what would become of her courage, Munday asked himself, what would become of her getting up and putting the sticks in the cold stove early morning after early morning? Why would she go to bed at night or why get up in the early hours if Ayton and he were no longer there? What sense would there be in sweeping patterns into the sand if there were only Quespelle's feet to walk over them? When they drove into the market-place in Le Havre, the dawn was just beginning to arch over the open square.

Quespelle was off to drink in the *bistro*, where the smell of boots and the smoke of men was thick on the air. But when it was full daylight, Munday left the rest of the selling to him and went off toward the harbor, seeking out Sophia to ask when the three of them would come to see them in the country. He walked down the little streets toward the masts that stood straight as iris stalks in the captive water of the harbor, his heels striking the cobblestones and awakening the life in his body. His throat filled up with stormy singing, with notes ready to burst his lips open, for now he was a strong, wealthy man walking the streets, and not a figure of grief and outcast. The ardor and the flattery the Church had given him was no richer than this wild elation from the heart and the mouth of another man.

He came to the side door of the House, and when he had rung the bell Sophia came to it and spoke to him through the half-opened door. Her hair was rolled tight on curling papers, he saw, and her voice was soft as a whisper. But in spite of its hush, Mrs. Sophia came running quickly on flapping bedroom slippers down the stairs.

"It's not a man, is it?" she cried. "It's not a man?"

"Yes, it's Mr. Munday," said Sophia.

"We can't have any man so early!" said Mrs. Sophia, the long, black, Spanish-like loops of her hair hanging over her sallow brow. "Who's Mr. Munday? He'll have to come back when the other gentlemen do, at a decent hour."

"But he doesn't want to come in, he wants me to go walking this afternoon with Blanca and Annchen," said Sophia, and then she was wiped aside as abruptly as if she had fainted, and Mrs. Sophia put her long jaw in the opening of the door.

"Not on a weekend," she said. "My girls are all in bed until after lunch. Such ladies. . ."

"Ayton is lonely," was what Munday said.

But when he returned to the cabin and saw Ayton twisting the pale flowers into shape for the dead, there was again no other thought in his head but what will become of Leonie? They were her reason for making the coffee fresh every morning, and for cutting the potatoes to fry one day as thin as ribbons and the next as thick as your thumb. She was standing in her clean blue dress, turning the sauce on the stove for them; they had given her a taste for the food she set on the table for them, and when they went on to the next place they would leave behind them their gratitude to her.

"Do you know, Munday, what the holy nut of England is?" he asked. You could look all over his face, and it would seem a fair enough face but when you came to the eyes you would pause and ask him to repeat again what it was he had just said. Munday sat down on a stool by the geranium shoots and watched him working. "It's the acorn," Ayton went on with it. "It would be nice to have just a little bit of England to carry around in my pocket. 'Britannia, upon your possessions the son eternally, the SUN, damn ye, eternally sweating!' Do you think I could write to Edith," he asked, "for the acorns I left at the house?"

"But it's probable they're watching her letters, you know," said Munday.

"I wouldn't have to tell her a thing," said Ayton. He wound the ribbons of raffia savagely about the flower stems. "Just *poste restante,* Montivilliers."

"But you'd have to give your name," said Munday.

"Unless you gave yours," Ayton suggested. "Risking a great deal," Munday said, "for the sake of a few acorns."

"I know, but I want to plant them," Ayton said.

They were silent for a while, and some light of the sun seemed striving to break through the heavy day. Munday could feel the tentative warmth of it on the glass behind his head. And then he said:

"I saw Sophia this morning, Ayton. I think the three of them will come."

"Ah, you're good to me!" said Ayton, and he looked with his shy, sly look under his lids at Munday. "If only you had your piano here, that would be the least I could do for you." But still he spoke casually of it, as though it were of no great moment after all. "You might have time to play it in the evenings at least, mightn't you?"

"I saw my music-box today," Munday said.

"No" said Ayton, and he put down the handful of flowers. "You went to your room, did you?"

"After the market," said Munday.

"Ah, what did you do there?" asked Ayton.

"I went to see my piano," Munday said, and he smiled.

"Did you play a tune?" Ayton asked.

"No," said Munday. "No, I didn't play."

"But how could you go that far and not play a tune?" cried Ayton. His light eyes were as clear and seemingly as fragile as glass.

"No," said Munday. "I didn't so much as open it."

"Then why did you go there?" Ayton asked sharply. Because he could not understand it, he felt small and thwarted as he tore apart the pallid flowers. But in a moment he turned again on Munday. "Did you go there alone? Maybe it was because you had someone with you?"

"I went there alone," said Munday, and he stood up and reached his hands high to the beam above his head. He closed his strong wide hands on the weather-grayed wood and lifted himself from the floor and swung back and forth. "You speak to me in censure as a woman might," he said.

"Ah, very well," said Ayton, "but you yourself know nothing of women."

"That's true," said Munday.

The comfort had gone from his heart now and he walked out into the garden, his hands clasped behind his back as he followed the pathway. His eyes were lowered to the ground, and whichever way they fell he could see the wondrous change that his and Ayton's work had brought upon the soil. The beds were clean and shapely now that the weeds had been torn from them. The stems of the tomato plants were clear and strong in preparation for their eventual bloom; he saw the earth that had been freed from stones taking its ease with the few straight stalks it had to nourish. And far away in the village he could see Rochereau's house, small and smokeless against the beginning of the woods. Rochereau, thought Munday, and he knew that however he himself changed from musician to laborer, from priest to sinner, day in and out the old man's unfaltering identity remained steadfast. How's your identity getting along, Mr. Munday? he asked himself. It's taking its ease for awhile, he answered, like the soil we've turned out fresh for planting.

As he walked on the path, with his eyes cast down, he came suddenly face to face with Leonie, as two monks walking in devotion might have interrupted each other's prayers and meditations. They stood for a moment silent, looking into each other's eyes, and then Leonie asked:

"What's the matter with Ayton," at the same moment that Munday said: "What's the matter with Ayton, Leonie?"

153

M UNDAY knocked on the door, and came in from the cold and sat down at the table, opposite the old man.

"I didn't think you would know me," Munday said.

Rochereau lifted his hand to his chin. "Because of the beard? Oh yes, I knew you at once."

"I've been away," said Munday.

"You wrote me from Mont St. Michel," Rochereau said.

Beside him the window looked out on the yardway that had been plucked clean of leaf and blade by the fowl that he kept here. The birds were stepping wanly about the barren place, pinning their eye-sight first to this and then to that, lifting their coarse feet like ends of yellow, knotted rope, and spreading them carefully on the ground again.

"Rochereau," said Munday, and he picked up a pencil to keep his fingers still. "How serious a matter is it if a second-mate on a ship, for instance, takes things, for one reason or another, from that ship, things he has no right to?"

The old man took the time to lay the tips of his fingers together.

"From the French merchant marine?" he asked.

Munday looked away out the window.

"No from the British," he said.

Munday watched the old man double his right hand into a fist and bring it down on the table.

"What have you to do with the British?" he cried out, and the frail old withered chin jutted forward under the loose lip. "In an Englishman a soul does not grow of itself," he stormed. "Sometimes he acquires one, but it is artificial, like an orchid made to bloom. Have you a friend without a soul then?" he enquired bitterly.

"No," said Munday. "I was educated for the priesthood, but still I could not tell you what a man's soul might be. But one day," he went on, "you asked me about my father, and now I can tell you what a fear he was to me. He was the kind of man," he said, choosing his words with care, "who was always going to come to life someday, sometime in the future, when this or that had taken place. But day after day we might have been living with a corpse for all we knew of him. There he was like a warning given me, the poor man shut up in himself with no action to declare himself, and never a word to let the cat out of the bag, or even to let us know if the cat in the bag was still alive." Rochereau sat quietly there, his red, bleak eyes not moving from Munday's face. "It may be," Munday went on, "that a man's right soul is his anger. My father never had any anger. He had no interest or heart for anything, and there must be some explanation for it. Someday he was going to start to live, and before he knew it the poor man was dead. He had no idea that one thing set on top of the other makes the monument. In spite of himself, although he'd had none of life, there was the monument piling up and there it was in the end. My father was nothing on earth, he was no one at all. But there was his terrible collection of privations building a monument of evasions. I want my life to be differently spent," said Munday. "I'll not hoard it away for safe-keeping, I'll spend it freely wherever I happen to be."

The old man's hands opened out wide, the fingers spread

on the papers on his table, and he leaned toward Munday, his voice growing stronger as he spoke.

"What are you doing up there with those people? What time have you to waste, with shiftless, Godless men?"

Munday saw the old, menacing figure at the table, one hand raised now as if in judgment on him, and the stern voice exhorting him.

"I have put righteous gods aside," Munday said, and as he spoke he felt the youth and the power of his love for Ayton sweeping through him. "For such gods are likely to ask a man to bow himself in remorse, and what is remorse, what is it but the faltering of the spirit?" They sat silent awhile, and Rochereau's fingers drummed on the table. After a little Munday said: "When I first came to you, it was about the gulls and the senseless slaughtering of them. And now I've come to you about something else."

But Rochereau's agitation was humming aloud in his throat as he looked away through the window.

"Where is your Englishman now?" he asked.

"He's up in the cabin," said Munday. "We met a *gendarme* last night after he talked with you."

"Well, then," the old man said grimly, stubbornly, "I'll answer you now as I did some months ago when you first came to see me, over there in the newspaper office. My opinion doesn't alter with the seasons. It is of no importance." He leaned forward and his faded, filmed eyes were fixed on Munday's face. "Whether or not your gulls are shot down, or whether or not your little Englishman is taken off to prison, it's of no importance at all"

"Could they put him in prison?" Munday asked.

Rochereau helped himself up from his chair. His legs were stiff from long sitting, and he pinched his glasses on his long, cold beak as he halted before the little closet of books. When Munday looked up, he realized that Rochereau must live alone in the house as a hermit lives, for the ashes were cold and piled deep in the chimney, and throughout the house there was no whisper of life. After a moment the old man came back to the table with a volume under his arm. He opened it out on the table and turned the leaves of it.

"'There are certain offenses,'" he began, reading the words in his high, shaking voice, "'for which the seaman is liable to be summarily punished under the Royal British Act of 1894. They comprise *desertion*—'" Rochereau kept his finger pointed on the word while he raised his head to eye Munday in rebuke. "'*Desertion!*'" he repeated. "'Neglect or refusal to join his ship or absence without leave, willful disobedience to lawful command, embezzlement or willful damage to her stores or cargo, etc., etc. Proceedings must be taken within six months.'" He read these sentences to Munday, and then he sat down abruptly in his chair, and his glasses ran down the ribbon on his coat and hung like shining eyes upon his heart. "If he stays out of sight for six months," he said, "there won't be any trouble after."

"There are the things in that valise," said Munday, "that will have to be got away."

"They should be given over to the Port Police," said Rochereau, speaking under his breath, his lips scarcely moving. "But if you should go there with them, it might get you into trouble. It should be someone strange to the Englishman—like a harmless old man, a Frenchman," he said, "a patriot, innocent of all suspicion—a man of standing, like Poincare—or me." But even as the old man said this, the meaning was so far from Munday's mind that he made no comment. "Yes," Rochereau was saying, "it would best be me who would do it. You tell me where the room is, and when the valise is with the port-men, it will be to see how things subside. Yes," he said, "but you will have to pay me for it! You will write three editorials for me, on the subject of the *Cartel des Gauches*. When I'm over there doing with the police for you, you'll take care of the printers over here—" There were papers thick on the table, and across the faces of them Munday's hand moving slowly to the sight of the old glazed hand that lay there as if forgotten amongst the written things. But it opened out as well, and Munday's strong wide hand fitted into the clasp of its ancient bones. So they sat for a little while, thinking of what had been said and what next to say.

But what will become of her, thought Munday as he came in from work that evening. If there were some kind of reward to give her, a perfume shop, or a pastry shop, or some kind of life to offer her after they had gone away. He came into the cabin, and she was cleaning Ayton's hair with Petrol Hahn, sitting by the stove with the supper smells escaping in mist on the air. Every piece of glass in the room in pitcher, or mirror, or tumbler, was frosted by the breath of whatever was cooking on the stove. And Leonie standing by Ayton's chair was shaking the rich drops of tonic out, so that the hair would grow thicker and brighter and stronger on his head.

"There," said Leonie.

"Are you done with me?" Ayton asked, his smooth bright locks combed back from his brow.

She set down the bottle on the table and went across the room to wash her hands in the basin of water. Munday watched her small hands turn the soap over and over in the water as she looked back over her shoulder.

"Yes, I'm through with you, Ayton," she said, and her eyes were soft with love.

CHAPTER XXII

B IANCA had a letter from Italy with bluebirds printed in flight across it and blossoms on the corner. It gave you such memories of the south, she said; of the bubbles that sprang up in the wine and of the candy virgins. A couple of licks, she said with a rip of laughter, and you had taken the Christ child right out of the virgin's arms!

In the middle of the kitchen table a *camembert* was streaming and stinking in its box, and Leonie had poured them out black coffee and put cognac in their glasses. Blanca read the letter out to them, putting the Italian words into French and sighing aloud for the sight and sounds and smells of Naples and Bari and Taranto. Blanca, Sophia, and Annchen had followed her through the cabin doorway and settled their backsides on Leonie's moaning chairs.

"My friend with a bust," said Blanca, "is crying for us to come to Italy."

"A bust of Caesar?" asked Ayton.

"*Ta gueule,*" said Blanca. "A bust of her own."

The tender Italian phrases slipped into French in her mouth, and Quespelle listened in silence with his feet on the stove and the visor of his cap tipped over his eyes. He knew not a word of any language save his own, but he sat reflecting as if upon depths of learning and perception, as if harking to so much that could never be understood by the others sitting there. There he lolled in his soiled blue denim jacket, a stubborn, thwart man, with his stunted arms crossed over his chest. The French language, he said, would always remain a mystery to a foreigner, for the similarity of sounds and the differences in meaning could never be grasped by the foreign, Anglo-Saxon mind.

"Take *vert*," he held forth, with the visor hanging over his muzzle. (Yes, muzzle, thought Munday. There was no other word to describe it.) "*Vert* is a color, but the same sound means 'glass'. Now listen carefully to this if you want to understand what I'm saying," he warned them, and he struck the words off on his fingers. "There's 'green' and 'glass' and 'worm' and 'poetry that rhymes' and 'toward' ".

"From the Latin '*vertigo*'," said Ayton. Quespelle nodded, impressed by this, and smiled condescendingly at the others.

"What can a foreigner make of that?" he asked of the foreigners at the table. "Or take the word—"

Leonie sat listening with respect to the size of his words and the deviousness of his learning, but her thoughts may well have been with the horse closed fast in the dirt of his stall, or with the neglected young lettuces and carrots far past their time for transplanting. She kept the guests' cups filled and the fire going in the stove, but it could be that she was thinking of the moment when Ayton and the others would remember all that needed to be done.

"My husband," she said at last, perhaps having seen the sullen look on Quespelle's face, thought Munday, now that he was no longer the center of attention, "He had an education better than most men we know. He even went to secondary school." She turned to point out to them the framed certificate hanging on the wall. "He was illegitimate, but he had a great father. His father was a lawyer." But still Quespelle would not follow where she led. He sat quiet and stubborn, looking darkly at her from under the visor of his cap. "His father used to go driving by in his own car," she said. "We used to see him in the evening, coming into the square in front of the cathedral and backing his car around, and getting out for the *apero*, with a big fur collar turned up around his neck."

But the forelegs of Quespelle's chair suddenly smote the ground as he sat up.

"He knew how to handle women," he said. It was afternoon, and the late gray April light coming in from the window struck the side of his unshaven face. For the words and the insult in them, he might have been giving them all a challenge. He was apart from any of them, throwing them off the scent, talking slowly and suavely now, but his eyes in retreat and the glasses of cognac tossed carefully, one after another, down his throat.

"He had no time for them," Quespelle announced. "He had his work to do. He kept his own counsel. He didn't go around telling everything he knew to anyone who put questions to him. You may be sure of that," he said.

He saw to it you were raised like a gentleman," said Leonie. "My mother-in-law was a *concierge*, and Quespelle was the lawyer's natural son. We saw him the day they got married, late in life, at the cathedral. There were twenty-five carriages following the bride and groom."

"He kept his own counsel," said Quespelle. "I was his son, but for all of that, he never spoke a word to me in my life. He had to keep hold of himself," said Quespelle, "he had to consider. He wasn't the kind of man who could afford to speak out all over the place."

"Quespelle was sent two new suits of clothes a year," said Leonie, nodding, "and given the best of everything."

"Not a *sou* did he ever give my mother," said Quespelle, and he settled his visor in pride. "He was too taken up with his work to give any thought to women. There were women all over Rouen who could have given him any thing if held lifted his little finger to them. But he hadn't the time. He had better things to do."

He settled himself back in comfort, ready to speak now, satisfied that the eyes in the room were turned on him. But suddenly Leonie turned her head and looked from the window, and then cried out his name.

"The cows, Quespelle!" she cried, and through the door they could see them trampling slowly through the garden with their strong split hoofs destroying and plundering as they advanced. They had broken through from the farm beyond on the plateau, and were coming down across the hill.

"Hi, hi!" Quespelle shouted, and the three men leapt to their feet and ran through the garden to head off the beasts. Ayton leaped nimbly over the rose-trees and the tough, dried, yellow ropes of cabbage, and down fled the cows in fright, moaning and hobbling, each with a foreleg tied to a crooked horn so that with every step they made their heads dipped low and their anguished lips struck their knees.

"Oh, *les pauvres!*" Annchen sobbed and down the hill ran Munday after the wildly bucking beasts. Quespelle's chickens flew up in the air, screaming at the lot of them, and goats reared out of the bushes, straining at their tethers. The chained dog was swinging on high like a meteor across the heavens.

Blanca stood by the cabin door, urging the men on, with laughter at the sight. But the tears stood out in Leonie's eyes for the trampling and stifling of plants and flowers under the cattle's cloven feet. The three girls, Blanca and Sophia and Annchen, stood laughing as the beasts went lurching and plunging down and the three men at their heels.

But Munday's laughter died in his mouth when he saw there was a woman climbing up the hill. Her head was raised toward Ayton in his wide descent, and as the cows scattered toward her she lifted a stick from the ground and waved it absently in the direction of their advance. He heard her voice ringing out in the mild spring afternoon.

"Ayton!" she called out in irritation. "Ayton, are you daft?"

The cows hobbled off to one side with their queer, crippled gait, and then Munday saw it was Edith who stood staring up the hill. Her face, with its small, sharp upper-lip, was set with her acrid smile; but no stream of true pleasure, or anger, or love, flowed under the surface of her skin. Her features were marked with recognition, but with little else besides.

"Hullo," said Ayton. "I was going to tell you I was here."

He stood still in the path, humbled, as a disobedient child might have stood waiting for the storm to break. Then he broke off a little spray of new leaves from a bush within hand's reach and struck his leg gently, rhythmically with it as he waited.

"Ah, you needn't have troubled," his sister said.

"Did you get the Black Virgin I sent you?" asked Ayton. "I sent it from Mont St. Michel."

"Yes, I did," said Edith, without enthusiasm, and at this Ayton took a step or two toward her down the hill. But then she said sharply: "So you deserted your ship, Ayton."

"Well, I know," said Ayton, "Well, I had to do that."

"You *had* to!" Edith cried out, and she gave a quick, hard snort of laughter. "*Had* to!" she said over the distance of land that still lay between them. "Oh, the cheek! The cheek!"

"No," said Ayton, speaking softly to her. "No, it is true, Edith. Can't you see how it might have been? Think of the time of the year it was, it was almost February, and I'd been a long time on the water. Ah, if you'd let your heart soften a minute, you'd come to understand," he said. "February's the time for other things, Edith. It's the time of a great change taking place in the soil in this part of the country."

And then he started going down the hillside, his small nimble feet shortening the distance between them. But Edith raised her stick in warning.

"Don't come too near me, Ayton," she said. "I don't know what I might do."

He stopped a few yards from her on the slope and he began saying in sorrow:

"It can't be that things would slip from your mind like that. I don't see how it could be. When we were in Ireland, you felt it the same as I did. And in the Highlands, you kept St. Bride's Day the same as me. If ever you've any feeling for the land, it doesn't go in a day from you. It's you and me who know best the life of the vegetation, we know the sleep the tree without leaves on it takes in the winter, and the rest that frozen water takes, are always the forsaken bridegroom and the forsaken bride."

On the hillside about them the spring was coming to life, emerging pale and feathery, but strong with youth, from the earth beneath it; it was the time of fresh new greens, and of the soil turned dark and fragrant.

"Maybe you felt it yourself at the start of February," he said, but Edith made no sign that she had heard. "I looked at the ashes in the chimney at Mont St. Michel in the morning, the way in the Hebrides you and I looked together, and just the same way the mark of Briid's club was there. I couldn't help myself after that," he said ruefully. "I knew the forsaken sleeper had been awakened and that the life of the vegetation was revived again. I knew it would be a prosperous good year then, the way it was foretold time and again for you and me."

He stood on the hillside with his wrists hanging out from the sleeves of his jacket, like the wrists of a young girl still slender and guileless and chaste.

"Two years ago," he said, sorrowing, "you made the bed

164

by the door on the first of February. I remember your standing there and singing: 'Bridget, Bridget, come in, the bed is ready!' "

For a moment it seemed that she would falter; she made no move, but she swayed uncertainly in the clear air. In time, she might have started running toward him, running with stumbling, dogged steps up the hill to him with her grief falling in tears down her face. But instead, she tossed her head up so violently that even her straw hat quivered.

"Ah, I don't remember it!" she cried out. "I don't remember!" And her hand was shaking on the stick she held. "I didn't come here to see you at all," she said, speaking sharply to him, "but you wrote me for the acorns. I would have left them at the Montivilliers post office just to get them out of the way. And what do I see but you flying down the hill—" She leaned over in her sensible tweed skirt and jacket and as she set the clean package down in the mud, her hat slipped sideways over one eye. "There're the acorns," she said, and she straightened up again. "There's one thing less of you in the house now."

Near to the cabin, the horse's long face was hanging out from the stall. Munday could see it nodding wearily and heavily at him as he climbed the path. But when the boulder of the animal's jaw was suddenly thrust upward, and the white saucers of its eyes began to spin he knew that Quespelle, coming from the other side, must be walking toward the stall.

In the cabin, Blanca had spread out the map of Italy on the table among the plates and the half-filled glasses and the platters of cheese. Here and there her finger went, picking out places along the route. Here the wine was good, and here the country was a vision.

"The only thing about it," she said in a moment, "is that we haven't asked Mrs. Sophia yet if she'll let Sophia go."

They were all of them coming to the table now, and Munday sat down to his glass of wine, wondering how

Ayton would escape from Edith, and how Ayton would make talk with them, and how turn his eyes away.

"She doesn't mind Sophia being in my company," said Blanca, and she reached for a glass of wine from where she stood. "But she's got this idea in her head about Annchen, that she might lead her daughter astray."

She set back the short lock of hair from her face, and then hung her thumbs from her hip pockets, standing with her legs spread wide apart in her fisherman's brown corduroy trousers.

"At one time I was very ill," said Annchen. "And, *figurez-vous*, Mrs. Sophia had a mistaken idea that I was trying to rid myself of something—of a little baby, *vous savez*."

"Was it Blanca gave you the baby?" asked Ayton, cleaning the mud from his shoes at the door.

"Oh, *pas de tout*," Annchen said, and her dark little face began to nod wildly at him. He had come in casually, with the package of acorns in his hand, and now he sat down lax and at ease with the others. "I was always Sophia's friend," said Annchen, and she shook her head sharply at Blanca as though the rancor still lingered. "I used to come see her every day through the side entrance to Mrs. Sophia's house. 'I've met such a distinguished young woman,' was the way she first broke the news to me. But I never for a minute thought of the truth of what was going on. *Aber nein*," she said bitterly, "I would never have thought of it! When she said 'I've met such a distinguished girl,' and started fussing with her hair in the glass I thought of a woman of learning and culture with a mouthful of teeth like an English virgin!" Her dark eyes were fixed in reproach and menace on Blanca, and the pale, strong woman herself leaned forward, completely composed, her features as though carved in the image of peace as she filled up Annchen's glass.

But once Annchen had drunk the red wine, the thoughts of what she had suffered became more than she could bear.

She twisted her hands in her lap and tried to speak of other things, but the memory of what had taken place had captured her, and one thought followed another in chaos in her head, at one moment boldly advancing and the next moment sliding backward into another time and place. She pulled her handkerchief out of her pocket and laid it against her trembling lips.

"*Et puis alors?*" asked Ayton maliciously.

"*Et puis alors,*" said Annchen. "One afternoon I went up as usual, and I knocked on Sophia's door. 'What do you want?' she said, and she sounded as if she was just waked up from a sleep. 'It's Annchen come to see you!' I said. And she gave such a cry, and she said 'My God, you can't come in now!' Her voice was so altered, I was certain she lay there dying. Her words were coming from a long distance, so it seemed to me, and her voice drawn out as thin as a string. I went flying out to find her mother, but Mrs. Sophia was out for a card game, and I walked around the streets like a crazy woman until it was evening." When Ayton poured the wine into her glass again, there seemed to be no sign of affliction, no scarring of her face, but she could scarcely lift the brimming tumbler to her lips. "I had a very bad time," she said. "I was *très malade* after. It was Blanca's fault, of course, but I've forgiven her for that long ago."

"There's no truth in sentiment," said Blanca, as she snapped her cigarette butt into the fire. "No truth in it. None."

"Well, I went back to the House cold to the bone, shaking, and my stomach empty," said Annchen, shaking now as she moved closer to the fire. "And I found Mrs. Sophia waiting for me. She says 'Sophia has found such a charming friend. Such a distinguished young lady from Strasbourg, like yourself!' I was ready to faint away, but I kept my self-possession. 'I let Sophia go out to the cinema theater to-night for once in her life,' said Mrs. Sophia. 'You'll be happy to make the young lady's acquaintance I'm sure, so come in tomorrow for tea.' I spent the whole night," said Annchen, "in going from one cinema show after another, paying my entrance and walking up and down the aisles to see if they were there. The ushers would try to make me sit down, or take my coat away from me, but I'd wait quiet there until the lights went up, or else I'd go along peering into every seat in the dark. If I found them sitting there in the theater, it would be all right, I thought. It would mean there was nothing going on between them. I would sit down beside them and start talking to Sophia. 'Sophia, why did you keep me out of your room this afternoon?' I'd ask. But even when I didn't find them in the cinema theaters, even then I had such a belief in her, I could not *croire*, I could not. It remained impossible for me."

She sat with her hands jerking in her lap, and her breath pulled sharply in and out. She must reveal all this to them, every word of it. Now she had become a caricature of herself, for all the functions of her being. All the words coming from her mouth, and the even beating of her heart even, were jerked into motion by a pitiless hand. "I went home in the early morning," she said, "after walking up and down in front of the cinema theaters when the people were coming out and the show over. But there was nothing, no sign of them. I would see a shoulder coming out of the crowd, or a hat with a feather like Sophia's, or a piece of yellow hair, and I'd be ready to walk up and hold out my hand to her, but it never turned out to be her. But at tea the next day," she said, "I told Mrs. Sophia her daughter looked flushed with fever. Blanca was there in the room as well, of course, and said 'Perhaps it's a bit of eye-strain. I've been teaching her how to do French knots!' Blanca had a cigarette in the parlor, and then she went off, and Mrs. Sophia left too for a game of cards. 'She's a beautiful young woman,' I said to Sophia, 'but that pallor looks unhealthy to me.' 'Oh, that's because she takes things,' said poor little Sophia, 'to give her pleasant dreams.' 'Was it she who was in your room with you yesterday when you wouldn't open the door?' I asked her. 'How can you say such things?' Sophia cried out. 'I had a sick headache and I was lying down.'"

Annchen was speaking with such rapidity now that Munday could scarcely make out one word from another. Her glass was empty of wine and her eyes were starting from her head. "Can you imagine, it took me a week to understand," she said, her voice gone dry in her throat. "I'd been two days knocking on the door of her room, and the first day I said through the door: 'Never mind, never mind, dear Sophia, don't disturb yourself.' I was beside myself with terror and I could barely get down the stairs again. But the next afternoon I came back again, and I kneeled down at the door, and I said: 'Sophia, dear Sophia, do let me in today!' And you know the door burst wide open, and me like a fool on my knees before it, and there stood Blanca. 'Come in,' she said roaring with laughter. She closed the door after me when I went in, and I saw Sophia sitting on the side of the bed with her hair all over the place. She was flushed from drinking and laughing, and there was a bottle of Martel more than half-empty on the table. 'You're a sight to behold,' I said to her, hoping this would sober her. 'Oh, Annchen we've been drinking,' she said to me, and she covered her face with her two hands. She was sitting there in her shirt, hanging her head down as if ashamed to see me. But even then I wouldn't believe, I couldn't think it. *Rendez-vous compte* of what a dupe I was!

"But suddenly Blanca pushed me off from where I had sat down beside Sophia, and she took her in her arms, holding her tight against her, the two of them in their *chemises*. 'This is what we were doing before you came in,' she said, 'like this, and like this.' She began kissing Sophia, and I could see Sophia fainting with pleasure in her embrace. 'This is what we were doing,' Blanca said. 'What are you going to do about it?' I jumped up and I said, 'My God, let me out! Let me out!' 'You can't get out,' said Blanca. 'I've locked the door so you have to stay here.' All I could see was that smile on her face, *vous comprenez*. I couldn't see anything else in the room clearly. I didn't know if it was night or day or summer or winter. I went around the room, running, and screaming like a jay. 'Look out,' said Blanca, 'you'll have Mrs. Sophia coming after us. If you don't like what's going on, try one of these.' She threw me a box of sleeping pills, and in the state I was in I thought I could take one of these pills and fall asleep there where I was, right at that moment. I kept my hand up over my eyes so I wouldn't see what was going on in the bed. But after I'd taken one pill, I could still see Blanca and Sophia clasped together. I couldn't move from it. I had to take all the pills, one after another. And after a while I fell over on the floor. I thought I fell on the floor," said Annchen, her voice rising higher. "But it was this way: when Blanca thought I was going to be sick, she took me out the door and left me alone in the hall. It's certain I fell down the flight of stairs after a while. It was already dark, it was the winter time, and when I got to the street, I fell right away into the gutter. I felt myself lying there a long time, but not myself, but another woman, a heavy, bloated woman lying there in the gutter. It was about four o'clock in the morning when some gentlemen passing on the sidewalk found me there and carried me into Mrs. Sophia's House."

"Poor dove!" said Blanca, and she lifted her broad hand now and stroked the side of Annchen's head. "I came in the next day, and I had to invent some kind of excuse to give Mrs. Sophia. So I told her that poor little Annchen had confessed to us her condition, and the fact as well that she had taken something to carry her troubles away. Then we nursed her there," said Blanca, moving her suave, gentle hand over Annchen's face and hair. "There we nursed her close and gentle, and the day I took her to her own house in a cab with me, we sat close on the seat with our hands clasped together, and by talking all the way to her I managed to overcome her unreasonable sorrow for the kind of woman I was . . . "

CHAPTER XXIII

T HE first thing that came to sight in the morning was
the arm of the tree reaching across the window.
Munday lay a long time in the twilight of dawn, waiting
for the low arm to swing out of the fading night and to
shake like a fist on the other side of the glass. The venom
and cavil of the intolerant were turned in this way on Ayton, he reflected, accusations and rebukes shaking in menace at him. And *hush, he has run a long way with the pack at
his heels,* Munday chided them and chided himself as well;
hush, *you must let him be.*

He lay gentle and still in the warmth of the bed, quite
apart from Ayton, who was turned away in sleep toward
the weathered planks of the wall. Like white moths coming awake in the cabin room, wisps of cotton that had been
stuffed into the knot-holes of the wood seemed to stir in
the semi-darkness. On the planks, pinned high, were
sheets of brown, store paper on which Ayton had drawn
the plans for the property. Here would the beans be
planted when the time came, and here tomato plants would
be set in, the furrows of pencil-lead marked where the
long, flowering avenues of peas would decorate the hill.

These things were becoming visible in the room, as well
as the faces and forms of women drawn by mildew on the
wood and the shape of continents inked in by the damp-
ness. But the room was clean, and it seemed a good place

to Munday. He asked no more of any room than that it serve its purpose; elegance in it, or polished boards under foot, belonged to other men and places.

To be young was enough in itself, he thought lying in the warmth of the bed. To be young, and to be enriched by his own new, physical power made his heart rejoice. It was there, tireless, endless, as he had seen it in the flesh of strong, young priests walking the country, walking, walking, as if to conquer the country itself at last. He had walked across England with them, and through France, and even if their faces were gaunt, this great stallion-strength in their limbs never lessened. But what release did they find for it, what bed-stream to cascade with the torrent of their passion? If they were like himself, then there was nothing given them beyond the swooning of the spirit in prayer. There was nothing, he thought, trying to go back in time, to remember; nothing, nothing worthy of the name elation, nothing to speak of the wild, blasphemous release that music spoke of.

It might even be that other men were denied any taste of it, rousing as they did to an unequal matching of their physical power. Or that a scarcely heard echo passed through their flesh, demeaned, as soft, wifely submission must demean so monstrously savage a sound. So he lay thinking, but he made no move, content with the exultation that now coursed slowly, drop by drop, in his veins. The days might seem alike, but he knew that each one had a different meaning to it. And now he told himself it was time to face the questions it would ask, and he got quietly out of bed.

On the other side of the timber he could hear Leonie grinding the coffee beans and the rasp of it on the air seemed violent enough to rouse the dead. But Ayton had not stirred, and didn't stir even when daylight began coming through the window. Leonie was sitting beside the stove with the grinder between her knees when Munday stepped into the kitchen, carrying his shoes for quiet, and silently closed the door behind him.

"Munday," she asked, "could you bring me back a little stick of rouge from town one morning?"

"Hush!" said Munday as he sat down by the stove to put on his shoes.

"Nothing ever wakes Ayton up," she said. She sat turning the handle of the grinder around and around, her hand firm on the wooden knob, her tanned arm bare to the elbow. "The Alsatian girls are talking of nothing but going to Italy," she added, and Munday heard the tremor in her voice.

"Yes," said Munday as he pulled the shoe laces tighter. Leaning so, he felt the color run down into his face.

"Maybe they talk a lot with no intention of going," said Leonie, watching for what his answer would be.

"No, I think they will go," said Munday as he sat up.

"And Ayton?" asked Leonie softly, her lips trembling on his name.

Munday could not bear to look at her, in fear of the anguish that must be there.

"Maybe we'll go along with them," he said, looking off through the kitchen doorway, but he could hear her pulling out the little drawer of ground coffee and tipping it into the filter. The last corner of dark coffee dust was so tenacious that she rapped the drawer severely with the side of her hand.

"Listen," said Leonie, and when he turned to face her she set the saucepan of water over the open fire. "You are safe here," she was saying. "Why should Ayton and you have to go away?"

"It would have to be sometime," said Munday. And then, seemingly heedless of her precariously unshielded longing, he added: "It's Ayton who wants to be off. He wants to get away."

He had turned straight on her, and spoke these words

174

without mercy as she stood looking into his shamed face, the grinder still hanging from her hand.

"Perhaps he's been lonely for a woman," she said.

"I don't think it would be that," said Munday, shifting his eyes away from her.

"Oh, men are sometimes very blind," said Leonie, and she set to pouring the water slowly, carefully through the rich coffee grounds. "You do not see things as clear as a woman sees them. And what kind of a life would you have if you went off, you and Ayton, together?" she asked.

Munday sat down at the table, but still he could not look at her.

"We could start off life somewhere else, in another town or country," said Munday, and for a startled moment he did not know if he were speaking these words about himself and Ayton or about Leonie and himself, and he quickly changed the direction in which the talk was going. "Rochereau's giving the things to the port police. In a little while Ayton will be clear and free," he said.

"Listen to me," said Leonie, and she sat down and folded her brown, young arms on the table top. "You don't know what you're saying, Mr. Munday. If you had any idea of what Ayton wants, Mr. Munday, you couldn't talk this way of him. Do you think he wants to be clear and free?" She brought him his coffee from the stove, and cut the bread for him, holding the loaf against her breast and drawing the knife straight through with such determination that it seemed it would cut into her heart. "It's a great excitement to him when he's in trouble," she said. "He'd certainly be the last one to thank you for your pains. He doesn't want his conscience made clear for him. You may not believe it, but I tell you it's true." She sat watching him as he dipped a crust of bread into his coffee, serving him and at the same time reproaching him, as only a woman could do. "Listen to me, Mr. Munday, listen to me," she went on, "You would go away and then Ayton would be a new kind of trouble to you. He can't keep still and quiet. You saw how it was with the acorns. He had to write and ask his sister for them. No matter what it brought on him, he had to do the thing he wanted to do."

"The things he does," said Munday, "they make him what he is."

"Then you must look out for him," said Leonie. "You must not take him to strange places." She went to the sideboard and brought him the jar of honey that was never brought down on any day but Sunday, and she opened it before him and heaped out the honey in lavish spoonfuls until it ran like gravy on his bread. "Listen, Munday," she said, sitting down again, "it's you must have the wisdom for him. He's such a child he has none of his own."

He saw her gentle hands folded, the nails broken and blunted from the savage and unending working of the soil. But her throat was tender and bare in her blouse, and her heart was pulsing gently there.

"No," he said, "even you would harm him if you could, and you cannot help yourself. He has never had a chance to live. He has always been judged. He has never been let be."

"But I understand his sister very well," said Leonie. "Listen, Munday, being here suits you. If you would stay, then we could make something good forever of the farm. I am sure of it. He is your friend," she said softly, "and maybe it is true you will pass your whole lives together."

"Ayton has no need to lie," said Munday simply, "not when he's with me."

"But maybe he wouldn't like that," said Leonie, "if he's got the habit of it. Listen, Munday, I couldn't bear it any more if the two of you went away. Look how the bush-beans and the little peas are blossoming!"

"How could you have the heart to do it?" she asked. "When you and Ayton came here, you made something else out of the place. I don't know what I'd do if you left.

I don't know what I'd do." She stood up from the table, and turned her head away from him, the soft shining weight of hair lying close upon her neck. Then she drew the back of her hand across her upper lip, across her nostrils, as she stood, turned away from him. "I'm feeling very sorry for myself," she said.

When Quespelle came in from the room where he had been sleeping, Munday drank down the last of his coffee and went out into the early day. By the step stood a wooden tub of clear icy water, and Munday ripped off his shirt and leaned above it, and the reflection of his head and bare torso fell sharply on the quiet glass. The white sky was mirrored deep in shadow below him, and into it he plunged his naked arms. He brought them up, aching with cold, and dashed handfuls of water over his head and his shoulders. All down his arms and on his chest he could see the tendrils of hair rising in astonishment. The day was so pure and fair that his sight seemed rinsed with it. He stood up, rubbing his bare body, feeling the blood in his face and ears warming, and when he looked up Leonie was standing above him on the step, as fresh and shining as if she too had been drenched in icy water.

"You'll get me a lipstick, won't you?" she asked as a child might have put a question to him, a curtain of tears clinging still to her lashes.

"It wouldn't do for you," said Munday. "Lipstick wouldn't suit you."

He pulled his shirt on over his head and buttoned it quickly.

"Oh, yes," said Leonie. "It would suit me very well." She came down the step and stood so close to him now that he might have put his arms about her. But she had no thought at all for him, thinking only of Ayton and of how her lips look.

"For when we go out at night, I'll use it then,'" she said.

CHAPTER XXIV

A YTON went eagerly through the forest, leading the way before Munday over the altering, melting ground. His pockets were filled with acorns, and into the earth under the vaporous web of leaves that lay rotting there from another season, he pressed the nuts deep down. This was his own drama played to the trees and the time of year; one by one pushed into the forest-soil, the nuts like notes of music, and the man's voice singing, exhorting the hesitant vegetation to unfold. Spring was a slow torment in the north, stricken now and again, and almost mortally, by a night of bitter cold, or held at bay by coupled days of deluge. But now that it was May Ayton must make this drama of urgency before it, must step this dance, cajoling it by imitation, describing by gesture how things should be.

"Now that it is spring," he said, going swiftly and eagerly over the deceptive soil, "now the time of waiting is over. Now the time has waned for men and animals to live in darkness, forgetting to reproduce their kind. The holy nut of England," he said, his nimble thumb pressing the acorns down, "it shall burst its shell and flower, and in years to come after the forests of France shall come to be thrown into shadow beneath you . . ." A red squirrel came singing over his head as he walked. Such a feast of nut-meat had drawn him from the further places of the forest and sent him winging from branch to branch with his arms spread batwise in his cloak. "Only if Death is buried under an oak does he leave us free, and Spring returns," said Ayton, "or Death may be flung into the water." Above him the squirrel clapped its black naked hands together in anger, hummed and swung above him, watching and waiting for a nut to fall from Ayton's pocket and be left behind on the ground.

"And 'Death swims on the water!' " sang Ayton. "Spring comes to visit us with eggs that are red, with pancakes that are yellow. I carry Death from the village, O holy Markets.' " he sang. " 'Now do I bury Death. Give us a good year for wheat and rye.' "

In time with this, Munday walked whistling like a bird, his head lifted to watch the swinging squirrel.

"Oh, I could give my whole life to guiding the seasons right," sighed Ayton. The day was cool through the boughs and through the scarcely-feathered crests of the trees, and thin clouds were drawn veil-like but complete across the sky. There was no reason to believe that the forest would ever be hearty and full again, or the undergrowth rich with green again. There was nowhere a sight of yellow, only the cold ebony blue of the needle trees, and icy lichen-flowers laid in white necklaces where the black rot of the trees' bark thrust up from the ground. This might be the long last twilight of the world and the end of it the night coming down forever. But still Ayton went on performing the ritual in hope, and in faith and hope bringing his clear, choir boy-like voice to bear upon the reluctance of spring.

"Oh, I could spend my best years showing the elements how to go or come or stay quiet," he sang in complaint. "If the shadow of the earth should fall on the sun or on the moon, I could drive it off myself with arrows. How do I know that the bushes will ever be green again, as green as they were once at another time, or how do I know that the pods will ever be filled again unless the way is shown them?"

Before them suddenly, as if they had come upon a charmed circle of land, they saw through the tree-trunks the Little Sisters of the Poor in their brown frocks running here and there in the perfect stillness. They were holding their skirts up from their ankles so as not to soil them as they ran, and their nuns' shoes showed under their hems, short and wide and decent, with black elastic laid in at the sides.

The Children of the Poor chased after them, beseeching the good sisters to be generous with them, pursuing them from tree to tree. Back and forth ran the little nuns and the children in pursuit, fleeing from one to the next of the broad-bodied trees. A pool of clarity lay above them, for here no boughs wove overhead and the forest had parted like lips in wonder. As they ran the Children of the Poor breathed in and out the magic air that hovered, uncommitted, between winter and spring.

"Oh, I should like to give them all pennies!" said Ayton, watching the children hiding in the nuns' skirts as they played, and shrieking there in soft delight and simulated fear. "Do you think I could run down and give them all pennies?" His fingers felt through his empty pockets. "Or acorns?" he asked, but suddenly the fury of being without a *sou* swept through him.

"I'm sick and tired of being a poor man!" he cried out. He looked bitterly at Munday. "I should be able to turn something into money. What of the things I left in your room? I've a right to them, you know."

"I'll give you what I have," said Munday, "as soon as the next check comes."

"But what about my pipes and my medals?" asked Ayton, his voice pressing gently on Munday who looked down through the assemblage of trees at the children's game.

"They've been turned over to the police," Munday said.

Without a word the little man went running past him down the slope and into the midst of the children. But past them too he ran, with his hands held over his head, and the children stood back in amazement. On the other side of the clearing he laid hold of the low bough of a tree and swung himself up and over. Over and over the bough he went, drawn up on his strong, shapely arms, and over and over, with his straight, pointed legs following after, and the acorns falling fast from his jacket.

Above his head an angry red squirrel flew from branch to branch, its tail turned up in a yellow feather across its back, and the hairs of its spine erect with rage. When the nuts poured out upon the ground below, the squirrel beat a tattoo of anger on the bough, and the children by the nuns' skirts leapt with joy. A squirrel scolding aloud in a tree, and a man going head-over-heels across a bough, were wonders they had never seen before.

Ayton stretched flat on the bough to catch his breath and then swam with his arms, slowly, like a man moving under weights of sea. But abruptly he dropped from the branch and sprang again to it before his feet had fairly borne his weight upon the ground, and the Little Sisters, the pure at heart, accepted this sight as they might have any visitation in the fields and stood murmuring together, speaking of his strength and grace as he spun around the flexible bough.

Munday did not look into the faces of the nuns as he walked down amongst them, and their attention was turned wholly on Ayton and they did not notice another man had come into their midst. He stood there, just out from the trees, watching the antics of the little man, and it seemed to him that with all that had come before, this must be a conjuring and rite as well. He stood watching Ayton, and he thought of the commands of the Church to the exercitant, directing: *to see with the eye of the imagina-*

tion, and to hear with the hearing what they say; with the sense of smell and taste must he perceive the immeasurable fragrance and sweetness of the Godhead, and with the sense of touch of the imagination must touch the places where Christ has set foot.

Little Sisters of the Poor, he thought, with such burning conviction that it must convey itself to their hearts, I love this man who sees holiness in tree or stone because even his principles burn to ashes in the flame of his desires. He is more simple and indolent than Christ, for even his own conscience is unable to be a compass for him. This holy beauty, it makes a belt of, yes, I say chastity of the spirit. Little Sisters of the Vain Poor, I shall save him forever from the onslaught of life, religion, love and the other things that encourage the soul to perish. If the exercitant must taste the loaves and fishes on the tongue of his imagination, then he must know whereof they come. For might not the bread be made to rise by music, and might not the fish be salted by the joys of the flesh? Little Sisters of the Outraged Poor, are you single at heart enough to receive a Master who carves your hands to His Will and who makes of your lives a white fan to cool the malice of the universe?

Once the blood was careening in him, there was no halting Ayton. He would be off, he would go on. He would descend the path beyond, wherever it might be leading him. He spoke no word of anger to Munday, but it was clear he had come to the end of his patience. He would be off and away. He would put his foot on the street of a town and let happen what would to him. They had taken the path time and again, but never come this far on it, and now he would follow it out to the end whatever harm it brought him. He would go to the end, and as he went swiftly along the path, he was flinging his words back to Munday, who followed at his heels:

"There's always some kind of taboo put on the best of men. The King of Leinster might not go round Tuath

Laighean left-hand-wise on Wednesday, nor sleep between the Dothair and the Duibhlinn with his head inclining to one side, nor encamp for nine days on the plains of Cualann, nor travel the road of Duibhlinn on Munday, nor ride a dirty black-heeled horse across Magh Maistean. And as for the king of Connaught, he might not go in a speckled garment on a gray speckled steed to the heath of Dal Chais, nor repair to an assembly of women at Seaghais, nor sit in autumn on the sepulchral mounds of the wife of Maine, nor contend in running with the rider of a gray one-eyed horse at Ath Gallta between two posts."

Down the steep path agile and quick he went, flickering through the trees like a minnow through water, and speaking out no word of rebuke to Munday but spending his anger in speech on the air. The fury for whatever it was, the thwarting, the imposition, came streaming out in recital, seemingly without a breath taken in between. He did not turn his head nor pay any heed to Munday's laughter.

"Oh, and the King of Ulster," it went on, over stone and root and the dry strings of forest-vine, "he was forbidden to attend the horse fair at Rath Line among the youths of Dal Araidhe, or to listen to the fluttering of the flocks of birds of Linn Saileach after sunset, or to drink the water of Bo Neimhidh between two darknesses."

So might a spring torrent have come cascading, skipping wild and whirling, with the bubbles cast back fresh upon the face of whoever followed behind.

"Oh, and the holy milkman," the voice of Ayton ran on, "must live at the sacred dairy and never visit his home or any ordinary village. If he is married he must leave his wife, and no ordinary man may touch the holy milkman even with the tip of his finger. The holy milkman may never cut his hair or pare his nails, nor cross a river by a bridge, but wade through fjords, and only certain fjords at that. Oh, and the wife of the Flamen Dialis must not ascend more than three steps of the kind of staircase called

Greek. . . ." But suddenly Ayton stopped short in his descent and spun about on Munday. "I could never understand how one man's conscience could work out for another. That's how I figger it. Once you start meddling in somebody else's life, where is it going to end?" A drop or two of rain fell through the branches now, and Munday felt the imprint of each of them, cold and gentle, on his eyelids and his mouth. "Sinning or erring," Ayton was saying in contempt, "I don't believe in it. You can't put things on me that I haven't any time for." His face was bright and certain while he spoke the words, but once they were said he looked in concern at Munday. "You've caught the habit from your religion, the kind of virtue that sees people all bad or else all good."

Munday came down the path to where the little man below him was dancing a jig of uncertainty on his supple feet, not knowing, it seemed, not quite sure how far he could let his annoyance go. For a moment he would let it spread, like a cloak unfurling about him, and then he would draw it in until there was no sign of it left.

"Keep such complaints to yourself," Munday said with his cold eyes on him. "They make you seem a pathetic, whining man. Your things are with the port police by now. That makes half a free man of you, but not entirely. There's that much off your mind, at least."

He dropped his hand on Ayton's shoulder, and the touch of it was as good as oil poured on water, suddenly the storm in Ayton's flesh subsided and left him standing there with no defenses.

"Ah, there's nothing taken off my mind at all." he said, both holding fast to Munday's arm. "I'm wild with fear, Munday, for what it might seem hard to imagine. It's for all the things that have been cut out for me to do in life."

CHAPTER XXV

THE days were warming now but even in the early hours, with the stars fragile and far in the dawn, there was bleakness in the air. Tufts of parsley, light and tender as maidenhair, blew against the ropes of cabbage beginning to go to flower, and by the side of the cabin there were rows of lettuce heads as elegantly petalled as orchids. Such was the early morning, and Munday the first out in it. He saw the dog's niche was standing empty, and this was so strange a thing that he halted awhile and stood staring down over the road and the valley, looking for a sight of the dog making toward the village or skirting the canal. It would be good to know that it had gone off to another life, had followed the Gypsies, maybe, his worn hide set free to wander, or starve, or find those who might cherish him, as no one had ever done. But once the watering-cans were filled at the pump and Munday was bearing them past the ardoises, he heard the dog's tail beating solidly against the timber of the horse's stall. Was it loneliness that had drawn him to seek out the company of the horse, he wondered. The steps in the garden must have roused him, and when Munday spoke his name now he came out smiling, his tail thrashing into action the grasses by the path. The dog followed him, gently and mildly wherever he went, standing near to him in the hot-house as he watered the geraniums, watching him sprinkle the new peas and lettuce plants with silver drops, lifting his ears at the sight of the curved needles of water that sprang from the tin's flat, perforated nose. Wherever he moved the dog moved on with him, blinking and swinging his tail slowly, patiently, as if in gratitude.

When the watering was done, Munday took the basket of parings from the kitchen-step and set off for the rabbit run. And everywhere, step by step, the dog came quietly after, his narrow tongue lolling out. Suddenly, in the increasing waves of morning light, Munday saw the white mother-rabbit lying in the grasses, stained with blood and torn apart, lying there gutted of her young. He stopped short and stood gazing down on her in shock and outrage, the fair whitecoated mother and her small ones torn out of her belly; and then, beyond her, four of the great striped Belgian hares stretched out, incredibly beautiful and seemingly unscathed, but dead as well. There he stood, waiting, as if for some explanation to be made by God or man.

He laid aside the basket of food that he carried and, kneeling, he began twisting the broken ends of the wire one into the other so that the still living rabbits within could not escape. They were crouched near the wooden hutch, motionless, their eyes still fixed in terror on the light of day. As Munday worked to close the opening, he looked in despair upon the glossy, lovely bodies of the slaughtered beasts. A fox or a weasel must have been out murdering while he and the others had slept in the cabin, unknowing, Munday reasoned. Some lusting assassin had committed this crime while they dreamed. When he had closed the gap in the wire, he ran toward the cabin, calling out Leonie's name, and when he passed the dog's solitary cell he saw that the dog had returned of itself to its shelter and was turning and turning about, flattening the tall, imaginary grasses within. He could hear the long coarse claws slipping and scratching on the boards, and when he leaned to fasten the collar again around his throat, the bony face was lifted to him servile and abased. But still no thought had come to him of the dog as murderer.

Quespelle was the first to come out, scarcely awake, with his visor tipped over his eyes. He followed Munday to the rabbit-run, and there he halted and began rolling tobacco into its paper. His arm came short and blunt from the frayed sleeve of his jacket, and the ends of his fingers fumbled the tobacco and the paper into shape, but still his mouth did not open, and even when the preparation of the cigarette was done, his lips did not part to take it. He seemed not to breathe for the while he stood there looking down at the dead animals lying at his feet.

"It must have been a fox or a weasel—" Munday began. But now an explosion of powerful derision transformed Quespelle's face. He looked in such triumph at Munday, in such contempt and such bitter exultation, for they had been a long time pitted against each other, and he had won out at last. He did not speak, but he turned back to the cabin, and through the doorway Munday could see him opening the barrel of his gun.

"What are you going to do?" asked Munday, and Quespelle came down the step and out into the yard again with the loaded gun in his hand, the cigarette hanging on his lip.

"It's the dog," he said. "If there's that in his blood, there's no way for it except killing him."

He talked of the dog, but he did not take his eyes from Munday. He stood, the gun in his hand, his hard little eyes on Munday's face and Munday began speaking to him, thinking his own temperance must alter Quespelle's intent.

"There's time to talk about it," he said, for the morning was still new, and far below them the sea was swelling in a clear, fragile bubble from the river's long, narrow cavity. "What's the use in killing the dog?" he asked, for outside, over there, he thought, beyond his own strength there must be some force vital enough to make impotent the other man's will. He stood looking into the valley, as if from there some help would come, but the houses, the ordinary, twin-like, coupled houses of the ammunition workers, and the lines of trees, were following the land's march toward the sea and had no time for lesser problems. "What use would it be to kill the dog?" Munday asked again, keeping the fear of failing from his voice and speaking earnestly and pleasantly to Quespelle. The dog himself had come out from his retreat and now shied from one end to the other of his chain. Munday watched the river grasses growing tall by the canal and the wind passing through them as if they were water, and he said: "There's time enough to talk it over."

Something will happen now, some decision come, he thought, but having taken his strength so long now from other places, he believed he was weaponless. If the Church, or some manifestation of it, would come to his aid, or if the landscape below would shift and intervene, the dog might be spared, but he himself was helpless. His own belief in the mercy and power of other things, in religion or in music he believed, had again betrayed him and left him abandoned, with no indication of what way to take.

"Stand aside," said Quespelle shortly. He had squatted down to take aim, and as if knowing there could be no help for it now, the dog fled back and forth on his chain with his eyes fixed on the man's threatening stance.

Of all the things there had been in his life, there was nothing, thought Munday, to prepare him for this brutal act. The Church and music had been his vocabulary, and he had turned to them for speech; but this time there were no words to cloak him, and the flesh might be taken from the bone, and the soul from the body, and no cloud conceal it, and no other name except murder be given to what he must now be witness to. But for all of this, the Church and music remained with him like two pale sisters laying their hands on him to quiet the outrage that coursed through his veins.

Because Munday did not move out of the range of the gun, Quespelle altered his own position and ordered Munday away. The dog had crept into its shelter again and its eyes shone like amber in the dark. A cry of anguish was shaking and rattling in his throat, in readiness to come streaming from his mouth when the gun would speak its single word.

"Stand aside," said Quespelle, cursing Munday under his breath, and he motioned him impatiently away. But Munday stepped close to him and lifted his right hand with the fingers curved tightly into his palm. He had no plan, but after a moment he hit Quespelle sharply under the mouth. The Frenchman stepped back and set down his gun, and when he opened his mouth to speak the blood ran down his chin. "I didn't know you wanted to fight," he said, spitting out the blood, and smiling fiercely at Munday in untroubled conceit.

"That's enough," Munday said. "Now just leave the dog alone."

But Quespelle came forward and lifted both his open hands, and seized Munday by the shoulders and shook him savagely back and forth, back and forth. Then he stepped back, eyed Munday, and with his right fist hit him on the jaw.

"There," said the Frenchman, and he wiped his palms on the sides of his jacket, smiling and reassured, believing the final word had been uttered. "There," he said, but Munday's fists sprang suddenly to life again and came dancing forward, racing together with their necks arched as they came. He felt the strength in them, and as he struck his mind went canny and crafty; in a little while he would get the dark throat of the Frenchman in his fingers, and whatever there was in that tough throat, he would have it out at last. He saw Quespelle rocking before him, waving like a strawman in the wind. It was breath in Munday's nostrils, the feel of his own hands cracking and smacking the face that went down on the clinkers of the path. But once Quespelle had fallen, Munday did not touch him. He stopped short, amazed at the sight of the man with his head turned sideways on the ground and the blood running out on his chin. The cap was gone, fallen into the flowers, and it was strange to see him with no covering on his forehead and the hair sticking thick as slime to his brow.

Munday walked off to the shelter of the *ardoises* then and picked up a bucket of water there, and bore it back, and flung it over Quespelle's face. He stood over him, drawing his own breath in and out, in and out, as if it were painful to him; and then he saw the Frenchman begin to move his head, begin to roll it back and forth, his mind returning from wherever it had gone.

Munday looked toward the cabin. He could not see Leonie but he called out to her, and as he raised his voice the hot bright air swung up and stifled him. He was giddy now with his own intemperance and he reeled across the yard and sat down in the shade.

CHAPTER XXVI

T HEY sat on the silky bottoms of the thin-legged chairs, Blanca, Sophia, and Annchen, and the wings of blue gas fluttered against the pleated crystal shade above their heads. This room, with the full-length mirror in one corner of it, was Mrs. Sophia's rendering of propriety. There was an elaborate explanation for virtue given quite simply in the candlesticks on the chimneypiece, chaste and white with baby-ribbons tied beneath their chins; and as well in the cotton petals of the nasturtium flowers under the half-dozen bells of glass; and in the clock that aped the façade of the Rheims cathedral, and in the red velvet hearts that hung on silk cords along one wall.

The game of "Solo" was theirs; it belonged to the women, and they had been many years at it. But for this time, in the nature of a maneuver, they had let Munday join them. Mrs. Sophia and the girls had begun the game, but now Munday sat at the card table as well. The cards were in Blanca's hands and she snapped them out on the inlaid ivory squares.

"He's good with the tools," she said, dealing out the almost worn out cards. "If you saw Ayton in the country, Mrs. Sophia, making little shelves for the corners, and stools, and making a picture-frame out of match-sticks. You know, always going in different directions."

"Pretty," said Annchen, nodding her head in confirmation of this truth.

"What a time you've had out there, sir," said Mrs. Sophia. Her eyes swelled up, bright and dark from the soft, white sacks of flesh that hung below them. "Living like a poor man, that little Ayton, nicely bred as he is!" She bowed her head to her cards, and the white hairs escaped from under her ebony wig and clung, beardlike, to her neck. "*Misere, abondance, solo,*" she said.

"Listen, Missis," said Blanca, "Ayton's one of the best." She picked up the *sous* as Mrs. Sophia paid them carefully out on the table. "But if ever the poor boy had a good idea in his head, that sister of his, if it wasn't her own, would take hold of it and disfigure it for him. Do you remember the tea-set he brought you that time from Dieppe? Well, she couldn't get her sleep at night at the thought of him bringing you a present. I myself heard the argument—he saying you were the most intelligent woman he'd ever run into, and she clawing at him tooth and nail—"

Mrs. Sophia sat listening in satisfaction as she played, but her glance was sharp with that same evasive, affrighted look of suspicion that Sophia herself reserved for the lot of them.

"He's a good boy, Ayton," she said after a little, and she let it rest there. But when she turned her mind to shuffling the cards, Blanca eyed her through the smoke of a tilted cigarette.

"A man knows best what another man's like," said Blanca. "Now, Munday, here—"

"*Misere, abondance, solo,*" Mrs. Sophia called out, and Blanca looked over at Munday and dropped one eyelid in what might be considered a wink.

"The injustices done Ayton impressed even such a scholar as Munday here," she said. "What do you say, Mr. Munday."

That was the end of June, and the women were dressed

in light things now, with their arms and throats bare. Blanca's arms were full and white and solid with a strength that seemed as relentless as stone, and Annchen's arms were also unblemished, although long, dark, silky threads of hair lay as if brushed with care across the forearms. Only when Munday glanced at Sophia's abject, pallid arms hanging loose from the sleeves of her blouse did the thought come to him as to what he wished to say.

"No," he said. "You, all of you, you know him better than I do. You, Mrs. Sophia, all of you. I don't know yet what reality is. I don't entirely believe in it. Perhaps it is only women who are born with any sense of what it is."

"You hear the complicated ideas he has?" asked Blanca. She spoke in a low voice, as though privately to Mrs. Sophia. "A student. A good influence for anybody."

"No, no!" Munday cried out. "I am nothing now! I am simply taking shape, I am coming little by little to life. I, myself, was put aside for a long time, and now I have to dream or remember how it was intended I should be. Now it might be that a totality has been restored to me. I can see only pieces of reality at any given time. I can see your arms lying there, different arms. But I can't see anything entirely." The women sat quiet, uneasy with this unusual talk. "Even when I hit Quespelle—" he said, and Mrs. Sophia looked sharply at him.

"Hit Quespelle?" she said in a muted, unfamiliar voice that was little more than a whisper.

"*Aber, jah,*" said Blanca as she passed her cigarettes around the table. "He gave him a thrashing. You should see the mug that he's left on him now. And all for what, do you think, Mrs. Sophia?" she asked, returning smoothly to the attack. "All for the ignorance of his lying tongue. He called you a this, and he called you a that."

"He called me a what?" the old woman cried out.

"He said he'd been to your house in the mornings after market," Blanca said, "and had been robbed, cheated, and misled. At that minute, Munday could stand no more of it and knocked him flying."

"No, no," said Munday, "I'll tell you how it was—"

Under the table, Blanca dropped her hand on his knee.

"Ayton's never been a mother," she said, addressing Mrs. Sophia, "but he might easily have been one the way he feels for a woman's troubles. But if ever he talks of another woman, his sister takes his head off for it; whenever he's with her he has to be lying and inventing until he's half crazy with it. I know how it's been when he wanted to come here and see you, she wouldn't have it. And now he wants to go off to Italy, but he can't tell his sister the truth. He can speak out what he has on his mind to you, but never to his sister. He can't so much as show his face in Le Havre for the moment, much as he wanted to come over with us tonight and have a hand of 'solo' with you. . . . "

Mrs. Sophia was pleased with this, and she lifted her hand to the back of her neck to tuck the stray hairs away under her peruke. Then she picked up her cards, turning the well-kept hands this way and that as if to call attention to her shapely wrists and to the lady-like knuckles that scarcely swelled under her skin.

"He's a good boy, Ayton," she said. She decided she would bake a cake for him and the girls could carry it out to him in the country. She was thinking of him as she played her cards. *"Misere, abondance, solo,"* she said.

"We'll have to get him away pretty quick, Mrs. Sophia," said Blanca playing the cards in the old lady's favor. "Things are pretty difficult for him the way they are."

"He's a good boy, Ayton," Mrs. Sophia repeated. "But what are your plans, Mr. Munday? Surely you can't send him off to Italy alone." The three girls paused in their playing, but they did not dare to exchange one with one another. Now it seemed that the moment to speak had come. Now, if ever, the time had come, but before Blanca could bring out the words, Mrs. Sophia again took up the conversation. "You and Ayton," she said, and her head gestured in grim satisfaction at Blanca, "you two have often given your thoughts and your consideration to what other young people only sneered at. . . ." She turned the last of her words in brutal savagery on Sophia and Annchen. "Before you and Ayton came into this place, I'd sit here alone with my cards at night, Blanca. . . ."

"But all of us, all of us," said Blanca, leaning toward her. "All of us came to you, *aber Gott*. Look at Munday here. He has his music waiting for him, he's a man with an occupation, Missis, he's an artist, *mon Dieu*, but he has no other inclination in life except to come here as we do and talk with you."

But peace and quiet was not to come as easy as this, for without a flicker of her black unswerving eyes Mrs. Sophia had turned taut and distrustful again. She held her cards high over her bosom so that the others at the table might not see, and she chose her words carefully, as if suspicious of them all.

"And Sophia is as close as our own kin to us," Blanca when on as a mask of smoke drifted slowly from her mouth.

"Oh, like a *soeur!*" cried Annchen, with a rush of hysterical laughter.

"*Solo!*" cried Mrs. Sophia. Her fingers hastened to scoop up the *sous*, evidently far more than she had dared hope would come to hand.

"Well, this is the way it is now, Missis," said Blanca. "Poor Ayton sits up behind a tree all day, if you could see him, in fear the police will come after him with a warrant for his arrest. He's afraid to come into the house to eat, and afraid to go to bed at night."

"The poor thing!" said Mrs. Sophia. She had laid her cards down now, and sat there, old and defenseless, won at last by the enchantment of Blanca's voice.

"If you could see him," said Blanca. "He carries the key to Munday's room around in his pocket, ready to skip at a moment's notice and hide, if it comes to that, until we can get him away."

"Oh, the poor thing!" murmured Mrs. Sophia. "The best way would be," said Blanca as she emptied the coins from her purse out over the cards, "for all of us to take a little jaunt with Ayton."

The girls and Munday sat like wax figures, on their elegant, brass-legged chairs, while Blanca, wary of their silence, was feeling the way the argument should go. But Sophia, hysterical with impatience, suddenly cried out:

"All my life, all my life, I have wanted to do exactly that kind of thing, but I have weak arches and I'm afraid I would be just a hindrance to you!"

"Aber, aber!" said Blanca, and she flung up her arms in impatience.

"What is it you've always wanted to do then?" asked Mrs. Sophia, her cold, level eyes turned on her daughter.

"Missis," said Blanca. She took the time to light another cigarette and then lifted it carefully from her lips. Now they could hear the band starting to play in the public hall. "I'll be twenty-one in a month or so, and I can take care of Sophia. We thought it might be pleasant to walk from here to Rome one day next week."

"Oh, you did, did you?" asked Mrs. Sophia. She put her handful of cards face-down on the table and spoke without anger. "Well, that's a fine idea!" she said, and she looked in condemnation at each one of them, bitterly, but sadly too, an old woman mutely beseeching a crumb of mercy from them, and the next moment she leaned over the table and hit Sophia across the top of the head. "That's what I think of your little jaunt!" she said, and Sophia began crying softly and shudderingly into her own hands.

Blanca jumped up, and the playing table tipped sideways with her violence; but she steadied it on its feet and, slowly, as if to subdue her anger, she pressed out the burning end of her cigarette in the pin-tray on the hand-painted face of Saint-Therese.

"God knows why Sophia should have to ask *your* permission, you old tart," she said.

"What's that?" cried Mrs. Sophia. "And what are you but no better than that yourself? And what has my daughter become since you've been carrying on with her?"

But Munday had had enough of it; the room was stifling him with the rising wrath of the women closed in it. He could feel it clogging his nostrils, and the taste of it had become poison on his tongue. He laid down his cards and pushed his chair from under him. He knew this was no place for a man to be. It was a house for men, yes, but now it had become a battleground of castigating tongues, the high-pitched voices whipping the air into a frenzy to the accompaniment of the band, the brass instruments clashing one against the other in a war of competition in the public hall downstairs.

It was then that the music Munday loved began to play, the notes singing in his ears with such power and beauty that the uproar from below and the voices of the women in the room were silenced. For now it was Mozart's *Don Giovanni* that he heard, and he listened to the duet and chorus as he had never listened before. Then came the soprano's aria soaring above the accompaniment of the clarinets, and the bassoons and strings, the clear voice asking: "Who can tell me where that monster is whom I loved, to my shame, and who was unfaithful to me? If I find him and he doesn't return to me, I'll tear his heart out, and make an example of him!"

"O, Lord, deliver me!" he said, and when he spoke Sophia slipped from her seat and onto her knees, soundless and limp, as a cloth might have slipped unnoticed from a chair. And now she lifted her voice with his, moaning and weeping. "Deliver me, O Lord!" spoke their voices together. Her hair had somehow unbraided itself and now it fell loose on her shoulders. Her pale eyes were wide open as tears coursed from them. But Munday's voice spoke in exhortation:

" 'By the rivers of Babylon, there we sat down, yea, we wept when we remembered Zion,' " he was saying. " 'We hung our harps upon willows in the midst thereof.' " The music of the public hall was growing more frantic, and the thrum and the thwang of the mechanical piano pounded against the ceiling of the room below. "How shall we sing the Lord's song in a strange land?" Munday asked, and the girl on the floor bowed in even greater agony and prayer.

"O Lord, deliver me, deliver me!" she moaned.

" 'I am like a pelican in the wilderness,' " came Munday's pure, exalted voice. " 'I am like an owl of the desert. Bless the Lord, O my soul, who satisfieth thy mouth with good things so that thy youth is renewed like an eagle's!' "

"O Lord, deliver me, deliver me!" Sophia cried as if in pain.

CHAPTER XXVII

J UNE was coming to an end in a stew of clouds, of sunsets red as carrots, of moons peeled off like onions. Every day of it might be the last, for the decision was made now. There was nothing to keep them longer: Blanca, Sophia, and Annchen, Ayton and Munday, they would all be on their way. Strong people they were, thought Munday; strong, easy people knowing what they had to do. Even Leonie, with her beautiful, patient eyes, seemed prepared for anything that they might leave her to face alone.

She was walking slowly down the avenue of bean-vines toward them, her blue apron gathered up before her in one hand, picking the beans off, first from one side and then the other. The last time, it came to Munday, that he might see her, with the dark tails of the bean-pods casting their shadows on her face. Or the last time that Ayton would stand in the shade under the ardoises with the bleached rope of raffia over his shoulders, preparing bouquets for the dead.

Quespelle was opening a bottle of wine under the beams and eyeing Munday. There was a difference in the Frenchman. It was scarcely perceptible, but different enough to hold his tongue quiet. If he wanted a cigarette from Munday's package, he would no longer speak out for it, so that Munday must remember and cross the shade to offer it to him. He had set out two empty glasses in invitation, but he would not ask the other men to join them.

The sun was sending strong white rays across the valley and Leonie walked back and forth through the light as if through shallow water. Beyond was the horseless cart piled up with the vegetable baskets, waiting. If he drove into town in the morning, it might be the last time too, Munday reflected.

"If a man hasn't this," said Quespelle. He made a shuffling movement with his forefinger and thumb and whistled softly. "*Allez!* Beat it! A woman will have nothing to do with you, that's a sure thing. You can just as well pack up your belongings and move along." Munday drank a glass of wine with him, nodding in agreement. The same bigoted vain talk listened to over and over. But there was a difference, as if Quespelle had gone deeper into his own bitter pride. "A woman won't give you much if you haven't the money to make it right for her," Quespelle went on, the insinuation of his talk falling drop by drop, like poison administered slowly on the air. There he stood, finishing off his glass and looking out over the summery garden. "Yes," he said, slowly, expecting no answer, no understanding even, "yes, she works for me, but she isn't a wife to me."

The sunlight was running in a shallow tide to the edge of the shadow, and Munday saw the crest of it shimmering and dry with dust. But because of the conceit now wounded and punished in him, Quespelle said no more. After a moment he walked away, dark, and short and dwarf-like into the sun. Leonie was lifting the full baskets of carrots and green beans, swinging them up over the side of the cart and settling them in place. The two of them were strong and fitted for any change, thought Munday; they could fend for themselves as they had done before. Any love she had for Ayton would decrease of itself, as a beast's dugs wither and dry without its young. She

200

would go on to something else, prepare for the next season, and for her it would come to an end that way.

But then as he looked at her, at her long dress and her apron crossed over her belly, another thought came into his head. He stood quite still under the *ardoises* with his empty glass in his hand. He saw her neck as firm and brown, and her cheek mottled with sun like a chipmunk's hide. There, from where he stood watching, the slim, young, shapely body seemed a moving sight to him. Her waist was thin as a willow, and her bosoms above it stood out in her dress like rich heavy fruit ready to break open.

He stood still with the empty glass in his hand, watching, and suddenly, as well as if she had come and told him in so many words, he knew what was taking place in her flesh. He saw her leaning to lift a basket, and her beauty seemed a pitiful thing to him.

"Leonie, Leonie," he said softly in reproach to her. He could not have spoken aloud, but still she heard and turned her face quickly to his voice.

"Eh?" she said, pausing at the side of the cart, her arms raised, setting the basket in.

"Leave the other baskets now," Munday said to her. "I'll finish with them."

But she was already up over the wheel to test the cart's balance with the weight of her body. She stood upright on it, warm and secret against the valley, swaying back and forth from her hips, with the light of the sun touching her hair to thick copper feathers across her brow. Munday walked close to the cart's wheel, and stood looking at the load, and at Leonie. Clear and perfect in his mind he could see the cabin in detail: the earthen floor strewn with sand, and the wind sighing through it like the boughs of a tree in the wind. He thought bitterly of all that was no concern of his now, but that was there to thwart them: pails to be mounted with water, the insistence of thirst and hunger, of soiled clothing and at last this new ravenous demand taking shape in her body. Her face was frail with weariness against the light, and for the first time she put out her hand to him to leap down upon the ground.

"Leonie—" he began. But he could say no more after, but held to her soft fingers. She looked closely at him, curiously into his face with her color mounting. "Something has happened to you, Leonie," he said with the breath that was left to him.

"Yes," said Leonie. She smiled at him and put her hand to her side in confusion. "I didn't know it could be noticed yet."

"But you can't do it, Leonie!" Munday cried.

"Why can't I?" she said. "Other women do."

"But you need things!" said Munday, speaking almost in grief. "You'll need money, and a place to be taken care of! You'll need not to work like this. You're not a peasant with generations of strength behind you!"

His eyes were fixed on the full blue veins that swelled on the backs of her hands and the mark that her wedding-ring had left, as if the flesh of that finger had been lashed tightly in.

"It won't happen for a long time," she said. "It will be winter. Things may be different then."

But what will become of her was the thought moving in grief within him. How will it happen with none of us there to ease her? And the storm of his anger and hate for Quespelle gathered in him again. What will become of her he was thinking in desperation when the three Alsatian girls came climbing up the hill. They went into the cabin and when Munday and Leonie followed them in, Blanca tossed her cloak aside.

"Leonie, my love," she said, as she kissed her. "You're as beautiful as an empress."

"I'll get some radishes," said Leonie, "to eat with the bread and wine you were good enough to bring us."

She went out through the cabin doorway, wiping her

hands off in her skirt. And "what's to become of Leonie?" asked Munday suddenly of Blanca, who was standing by, lighting a cigarette, and of Sophia and Annchen.

"Sapristi! What became of her before we all came out here?" said Blanca as she tossed the match into the lighted stove.

"You don't want to take her along to Italy too, do you?" said Annchen with a gasp of laughter.

"But what will become of her if we leave her here?" Munday asked, and Blanca shrugged her broad shoulders.

"I couldn't say."

"She won't be able to bear it," Munday said softly. "She'll be too lonely—" But Leonie had come back amongst them now with the muddy roots of the radishes hanging from her hand. She thrust them into the water that stood in the pail and with the flat of her thumb rubbed the firm red buttons clean.

"Ha, ha," said Blanca, "I've never been lonely in my life! *Aber Gott,* Munday! My trouble has always been to get some time to be alone!"

They opened the bottles of wine and set the fruit out on platters, but Munday could find no other words to say to them. Sophia and Annchen began their knitting, and in a moment Quespelle came in through the doorway and touched his cap to the company. He sat down without a word and began to eat the soup that Leonie put before him. Munday watched the jaw shifting under the brimming spoon and the soup running through the stubble on Quespelle's chin unheeded until he wiped it off on the back of his hand. His neck was seamed and scarred with dirt, and however good his soul might be it was sewed up tight in a coarse filthy skin. Maybe he was a sad defeated man with his own tragedy alive in him, but in his hate for him Munday would have liked to see him dead.

Then Ayton came into the cabin and the conversation

altered. He came stepping lightly, clean as a lark, into the last sunlight in the cabin room.

"Hello," he said. He went to the basin to wash his hands, talking over his shoulder to them, fair and young, and shy-seeming, as other men had not the grace or the time to be. "It's finished up," he said. "Everything in, and as neat as knitting."

"Then his elegance is ready to blow?" asked Blanca.

"Yes," said Ayton. He dried his hands on the cloth that hung by the window. "I'm ready to blow."

"Ayton," said Munday, but now the three girls had started the talk of Italy going around the table, and no one seemed to hear him speak.

"Next winter there'll be the Scala in Milano," said Blanca, filling, Munday's glass again. But Leonie turned her face to him in entreaty; and no, he said under his breath, no, and he shook his head at her. No, he said with his lips and his eyes speaking in silence. No, we will not leave you behind. There must be a way, he said, and his hand reached out and touched her fingers. No, he said silently, it is not possible to leave you here.

CHAPTER XXVIII

T IENS!" said Leonie, with her head lifted. Now that it was dark and the lamp lit, someone could be heard coming up the path, and the dog barking at the end of his chain in warning. "*Tiens!*" said Leonie, for someone could be heard rapping at the wood of the cabin, knocking at the timber in the absence of any door.

They all sat at the table, as if transfixed, and then Leonie rose to her feet and crossed the room to the window. It was almost dark, but some shape or color she saw through the dim little panes made her start back. Her hand flew up to the side of her face, and she swung about to the others sitting watchful in the lamp-light.

"It's the police," she whispered to them. There was the soft, rapid murmur of their voices, but Munday did not lift his head. He looked steadily at his own hand that lay on the edge of the table, and at the length of ash burning slowly longer and longer on his cigarette.

"Don't move, Ayton," he said to his hand. "Just take another drink. Let them come in without a word, Ayton." He turned his head to Leonie. "Why don't you ask the gentlemen in?"

Leonie moved uncertainly to the doorway, her hand trembling. She lifted the sack-cloth aside and stared out at them.

"Good evening. What do you want?" she asked.

"Good evening, the company," said the *gendarmes*. In their trim little hats and their fitted suits, they walked into the clean, poor kitchen where the group of motionless people sat. From the figure and the cut, either of the neat little men might have been taken for the other; but one was as swarthy as an Italian in the face, and the other was the same blond *gendarme* who had lost the saucepans on the night of the play.

Quespelle set down his chair on its forelegs and stood up, holding out his hands to them in greeting: to one his left hand, and his right hand to the other.

"Sit down and join the company, gentlemen," he said.

But they had no use for the handshakes he offered them.

"We're not out this evening for the sake of the promenade," the dark officer said. He was holding a paper in his hand, rolled hollow and long like a clinical tube. The other looked over the faces at the table.

"*Bien*," he said with a sharper look when he came to Munday. "You and I have met before!"

Munday stood up and shook his hand.

"And your friend there?" said the *gendarme*. He pointed his chin at Ayton. "I thought he was off to England with his saucepans?" He looked quickly around the cabin, and spied them at once, with their shiny bottoms up, hanging along the wall. "*Bon Dieu!*" he said bitterly. "There they are, the saucepans!"

He touched the other *gendarme's* sleeve and pointed them out. "There are the saucepans I told you about!" he said grievously. "Look at the wooden handles!"

But the other was set on doing his business. He was newly married and in haste to be getting home.

"We've served notice on you before, Quespelle," he said.

"On what grounds?" said Quespelle. He poured out two glasses of wine for them, but they made as if they had not seen.

"You've got a dog outside without a license, you've no

permit to sell comestibles in market," said the officer. "And you have no right to be living on this property at all."

"I'm no producer," said Quespelle, still smiling. "I grow a few vegetables for the people who live here with me and for a few friends in Le Havre."

The *gendarme* with the tube of paper in his hand looked gravely around the table and nodded.

"I'll have a look at their papers afterwards," he said. Then suddenly he turned on Quespelle's smiling ways. He wanted to have it over with and get home to his bed. "Now enough of this!" he shouted. He brought his hand down on the table. And "*aber*, my good man," said Blanca mildly, "spare the food and drink, will you?"

"You're a thief and a liar, Quespelle!" cried the dark man. He would shout Quespelle into submission. He wanted to get home. He was late enough as it was. "You're on land that is not your property!"

"Nor yours either!" shouted Quespelle. "I know the law as well, if not better than you do! My father was more honest than any of you, a lawyer he was! The police can't touch me on this ground unless the owner of it brings suit against me! And even then you can't put me off! There's no man alive can rightly put me off until I find another habitation!"

The two of them were staring in transport at each other's faces, their black chins so close that the ends of their mustaches came near to touching. But in a moment the *gendarme* straightened up, bit his lip and shook his head patiently at Quespelle.

"You can't get away with it," he said. He took a turn across the sand of the kitchen-floor. "It happens," he said, presently, "that the owner of this land has protested. Mr. Rochereau had an article in yesterday morning's paper—"

"Rochereau?" said Munday.

"Yes," said the *gendarme*. "If any of you had any education you would know the name."

207

"Education?" said Quespelle, and he sat down on the table's edge and folded his arms over. "Education? You talk to me about education?"

He swung his leg out before him in weary, amused contempt.

"And if any of you had any education," said the *gendarme*, halting in wrath before him, "you would have read the article Mr. Rochereau wrote. He said that this, this kind of thing, was a disgrace to the nation and that it was high time steps were taken to prevent outsiders coming in and appropriating the land!"

When his voice had ceased, Munday stood up with his hands in his pockets.

"But I don't understand, I don't understand it," he said. He looked from one *gendarme* to the other, and the dark one shrugged his shoulders.

"Whether you do or whether you don't," he said, "it all comes to the same thing. This land belongs to Mr. Rochereau. He owns all this side of the hill."

But now the blond gendarme began to play his part in it. His blue, unhappy eyes rolled vaguely over Munday's features. He was not malignant, nor angry even, only wronged and aggrieved. He did not want too much of them, he himself, only some small thing in reprisal.

"What is this settlement up here anyway?" he said. "How do you all of you explain your being here?"

"But why should we explain?" cried Ayton, jumping to his feet.

"*Aber,* sit down," said Blanca, wearily.

She sat him down by one casual hand pulling the tail of his coat. But up he shot again like a jack-in-the-box.

"I can't see why we should have to explain anything to you," he said. "It's impertinent on your part to ask."

The blond *gendarme's* face began to glow now, began slowly to kindle, as if the cloud of stupidity that had masked it were dispersing.

208

"That's the one who got away with the saucepans," he said.

"Let us see your identity papers," said the other officer, and one by one, like a game of cards the passport books were laid out on the table. The two *gendarmes* reached at once for Ayton's, and the dark one got it first in his hand.

"It doesn't look very much like me, does it?" said Ayton. He stood by the officer's arm looking quizzically, guilelessly down at the open page.

"It doesn't look like you at all," said the blond one. There was no suspicion, only grave, doltish wonder in his face.

"I know," said Ayton. "A passport photograph is the most unflattering thing in the world." "It says 'hair, chestnut,'" said the dark one, looking sharply at him.

"I know," said Ayton. "That's the way they are. But my hair was some darker then. I'd put something on it, just to give it a try. But it didn't suit me."

"Is your name John Harpy?" asked the blond *gendarme*.

All these things seemed to come slowly, thickly, in the direction of, but never quite reaching, his mind.

"They insisted on writing that name there for me," said Ayton. "They got it off my birth certificate or somewhere, and wrote it down."

"Then your name is John Harpy?" asked the dark one looking sternly at Ayton. It was just coming into his head that the English were trying to make a fool of him.

Ayton started laughing, leaning back with his hands thrust in flat between his belt and his belly. "No one's ever called me 'John Harpy,'" he said.

The two men in uniform could make nothing of it; they stood together under the light turning the pages of the passport over and over. So much of arrogance and ease was expected of them, and nothing save the neat little uniform had been given them in equipment. Because they were Frenchmen there was no memory of tyranny and inquisition behind them to make them domineering men;

they were soft as women in their hearts, and could turn with the same unreasoning, convulsive fury, but each of them had a small and human willingness to understand or to respect whatever might be said.

"We'll take it with us," said the dark man at last. And when he put it into his pocket, they went on to the other passports. "I'll telephone the Consul in the morning. You can come in to the *Mairie* and get it again during the day."

"But you can't go off with my passport," said Ayton. The color had gone from his face. The blond man halted and looked at him in slow wonder.

"Yes, we can take it," said the dark one, and he went on with the other papers, seemingly too engrossed, too lost in official duty, to meet Ayton's eyes.

"I'm a friend of Rochereau's," said Munday, handing his own papers over. "Rochereau knows us well. Perhaps you saw an article or two of mine in the paper."

The dark man stopped and eyed him.

"Of yours?" he said.

"In April," said Munday, "I took care of the printers for him—laid out the three numbers for him."

"Well, there's still the matter of the land," said the *gendarme*. "Mr. Rochereau has lost his patience. He kept quiet a long time about outsiders coming onto it, but now he's had enough." His face changed entirely when he turned it toward Quespelle. "We give you forty-eight hours, you," he said. "Thanks to your friend here, that'll be the end of it." Quespelle shifted his visor over his eyes. He put his head back, slow and steady on his thick neck, and looked at the *gendarmes*.

"No, you can't do that," he said.

The *gendarmes* settled their capes on their shoulders.

"This place has got to be clear of you in forty-eight hours," said the dark one. Quespelle's cigarette hung black and dead on his lip.

"You can't do it," he said. "You can't put a man out that way."

"You've heard me now," said the *gendarme*. He settled his belt and then he raised his hand and saluted casually in the direction of the table. "Good evening, ladies and gentlemen," he said.

The blond gendarme hoisted up his own belt and looked in dull, doltish stupefaction at Ayton.

"The saucepans—" he began, but in spite of himself he must follow the other out the door. And the cabin was left quiet, with the men and the women sitting there silent. From the calming of the dog's barking they knew that the *gendarmes* must be going off down the hill.

CHAPTER XXIX

H E did not know when he had begun to listen to the rain, but now he heard it striking aloud on the roof, falling, falling, each drop heard on the tarred surface, like fingers tapping for entry. It must have been after the three girls had gone out, and Quespelle had gone into the bedroom, ready to sleep as he was with his coat on and his visor down over his face. It must have been when the door closed behind Quespelle that Munday began to hear it, and he looked up at Leonie and Ayton sitting with him at the table. Leonie was smiling, for she was not afraid; now that it had happened she was not afraid any more. But Ayton's face had gone straight and narrow.

"Listen here, Munday," he said. "I don't like it." There were his wrists, fair and youthful under the light, covered with their down of golden hair. "I don't like it. I'd better be off. I'm better anywhere rather than waiting here."

"You can go along to Le Havre and wait for us," said Munday. "I'll come in the morning. You go along to my room and wait."

"I'll go with you on the cart," said Ayton. "I can't help it. That gave me a turn all right. Jesus," he said. He wiped his face with his open hand and his arm was shaking. Munday saw the dew on his lip, but Leonie was smiling uncertainly, for they had spoken in English and she could not be sure what they were saying.

"They've take your passport," she said to Ayton. "Now you can't go away."

"Ah, that wasn't mine," said Ayton. "That was the papers of a friend I used to have. There was a chap I used to know," he said, and his grin went suddenly stiff across his face, "in Hong-Kong." He wiped his upper lip again. "He got into trouble in a smoke-shop one night, and they gave him his proper, by God. But him being a friend of mine, I got the money and the passport they left on his body."

Then Ayton began to laugh—high, strange, uneasy laughter.

"You go to bed, Ayton," said Munday.

"I can't," said Ayton. "I can't spend the night in this house. I don't like it. All this," he said. "It's got me jumpy. It's got me thinking of Harpy. I don't like it. I haven't thought for a year about Harpy, and now I'm thinking about him again."

Munday sat listening, and it seemed to him that his own face and heart were altering as he listened. Ayton had left his chair and was walking up and down the kitchen, treading nervously on the sand of the floor.

"I'll make you some *camomile*," said Leonie. That will make you sleepy."

"There wasn't any sense," said Ayton, "in what they did to him." He kept walking across and across the room, and when Leonie put the water on the fire, he said:

"Listen. I can't spend the night here. "We'll go out and walk a bit," said Munday. He stood up and took his corduroy coat from the peg by the doorway and put his arms in and buttoned it over.

"Maybe you can tire out the devil in me," said Ayton.

"There's no devil in you," said Munday. But Ayton said quickly: "Yes, there's a devil in me. You'd better be through with me now before you see that its God's truth." They left the cabin together, and Ayton went on talking.

"If you still have one or two good thoughts of me left, then you'd better get rid of me before you have no decent opinion of me at all. I'm a sinner, and there's no denying it."

So he went on in a tragic, rueful voice, the fear almost gone from it now, but the stubborn, woeful complaint remaining. They were slipping down the side of the hill, a little apart, and Munday said:

"Tell me what you have on your mind now. It won't make any difference in my feelings about you."

"Ah, yes, it will make a difference," said Ayton. "It's bound to. You'd have to reproach me for it. You'd be sure of what I was then, although I never had the courage to tell you."

"You can tell me the truth," said Munday sliding down in the dark.

"Whatever I'm doing, there's always a devil in me urging me on to something else," said Ayton. "That's the whole truth, Munday, or as near to it as I can come."

There was a light shining in Rochereau's house despite the late hour, and when the two men came through the barren yard the chickens roosted under the shed shifted closer to one another, perched as they were muffled and headless in the light that came through the window-pane. The front door was standing partly open, and Munday pushed it wider. Standing on the threshold with Ayton beside him he called out: "Rochereau!"

Behind was the wet night, and before them the passageway of light out of the darkness. Munday paused at the edge, fearing for the moment to step into the other realm. The wine he had drunk all evening made each thought in his head start out in relief, perfect but fearful to him.

"Let's get on with it," Ayton whispered.

They went down the corridor until they came to the room where the old man was sitting at the table. His hand was on the tablecloth before him and he was staring into the empty fireplace.

214

"Rochereau," said Munday. "You might have settled it otherwise than by sending the police after us." But the old man did not turn his head. Dishes from his supper remained on the table before him. "Were you trying to save my soul for music or for politics?" Munday asked. In him was the confidence of being past shame so that now he could speak out as he pleased. If shyness or sentiment came up between them, he knew he would be able to handle the situation. "Rochereau," he said, "Quespelle has his wife and his garden, things to consider. He's not a man alone, as you and I are. "He has his wife, and he'll have a child in a little while—"

Ayton touched his sleeve as he stood talking.

"Tell him about me too," he whispered, "about the trouble he's made for me."

"If you could only have it all put off for a little," Munday said into Rochereau's silence, and then his hand closed over the old hand lying on the cloth. And now, as though it had been a long time cooling, Munday's tongue froze in his mouth. The hand under his was stiff as carrion. The eyes before him were looking into his face but through it and far, far out beyond. Munday pressed the old man's shoulder, and the bone in the coat was sharp and inflexible as iron. *So you need not answer,* he thought craftily. *So you got out of it very well.*

There sat the old man stonily in his chair, eyeing the empty fireplace sadly; a corpse, incongruously dressed in coat and breeches, sitting before the hearth.

"He's dead!" said Munday.

He could scarcely cross the room in his agitation, and then the two of them left the house. Down the steps and through the yard and out into the streaming invisible road they went through the darkness and the rain. Up the hill they climbed with no sense of time or haste. The night did not seem an interval: it was a dark, pouring torrent of water and wind that swept past them, carrying trees, thickets, and tangled refuse with it. They could not stem nor breast the current but must climb, sightless, from branch to root and whatever foothold held to in passing.

They had come through the forest in the valley, and the great flood of drowning night seemed to hurl the trees mightily past them. Nothing could halt the torrent of night in its thunderous descent. The thought that took shape in Munday's head, bobbing like a cork on the surface of his thinking, was that to reach their destination they must yield to the swift rapids. Then they might be cast at last on a calm and quiet shore.

But to see without sight the darkness treed and stoned was far more than had he seen what truthfully was there. He paused, breathing hard, waiting for Ayton to catch up with him while the roots of trees dripping tar and earth, and clots of meadow-grass came sweeping in between them.

"The last man I ever saw dead was Harpy," said Ayton, breathing hard. "There's never been anyone like him. I wouldn't be what I am now, with no real blood in my veins any more, if it wasn't that they killed Harpy. They didn't have to do it. He wasn't thirty yet. There was no need for them to do what they did. They all have the same look when they're dead'" he went on with it. "Awful. Harpy had it. Another look on his face, like a virtuous man, nothing to do with Harpy."

But Munday said no word in response, but heard these things in silence. "He was born twice," said Ayton out of the darkness. "You can be sure of that. He wasn't any ordinary man. Maybe he'll be born again. That can't be the end of him. Death was no kind of an end for Harpy. He used to say he'd take all the things he wanted with him: like his pistol, and his mate's whistle, and the things that he'd be needing. Maybe I ought to have left his money on him at that."

"And his passport," said Munday bitterly.

"No," said Ayton, "I knew he'd want me to keep it for him. He had a very good idea about how it would be, about the messenger of Death coming in a kind of glass boat, represented by a beautiful but evil woman. Then he'd go off with her, and in the Place of the Dead some other body and soul might be given him. Then he might come back again, the way he was twice born before."

The storm and the night were almost spent, and Munday's mouth was sick with the taste of surfeit. From the first it must have been so; from the first day, since always, this hastily and incompletely covered corpse had been lying under its loose shroud in Ayton's heart. But still the voice went on, blind, impersonal, removed a little now from grief.

"He had no ordinary ideas about life," said Ayton. "Here's what he used to say about it: 'It's the field of age, the mountain of youth, the chase of ages after the king in the house of earth and stones (that means the earthly world), between the candle and its end, between combat and the hatred of combat (that is, to the light, and during the struggle for life until the end of life and the peace of death, that peace which one attains to).'"

The night was over with now, but there was no sign of the gray weather changing. The shapes of the trees were beginning to show, and the line of the Montivilliers road began coming clear. The gloom of night was rolling steadily away up the valley, like smoke blowing from a smoldering fire, and ducks, flying high, went inland in formation. Munday could not see them, but he could hear them passing, as a planet of other life might pass low and the faint cries from it come drifting down.

"Why have they all the same look when they're dead?" asked Ayton. Munday could see him in the half twilight now. The hysteria and the anguish were apparently gone, and it seemed there was nothing more to say. But "What do you think killed the old man off?" said Ayton.

"Maybe it was his heart," said Munday.

And suddenly Ayton said: "Maybe the police will put this on us, too, Munday. You'd better let me skip without you."

"That's not reason enough for us to go separate ways," Munday said.

They were almost at the cabin, climbing close to each other, without speech. In the yard the cart would be loaded with the baskets of new lettuce, cold with rain, and with baskets of fresh carrots. The tall, blue grass of the fields was deep and drenching as they walked, but the rain could be seen still, as it drew away across the hills.

Once in the cabin, Quespelle and Ayton sat eating bread and drank their coffee in silence under the lamp-light, but Munday followed Leonie out into the dim light of the dawn. She paid no heed to him, but led the horse from its stall and backed it into the shafts of the wagon, and, as the shafts lifted, the high pale load of baskets swung slowly downwards. Long wisps of mist were lying over the river, blotting, and revealing, and blotting out again the lanterns of the ship, but what animals there were on the hill, such as the hares waking and thumping their hind legs on the ground, and the goats beginning to bleat, were muted sounds.

"You don't know what may happen to him," said Leonie, as she fastened the buckles of the horse's harness.

"He'll be better in the city," said Munday. "I'll stay the day in town with him and come back in the evening."

In another minute Ayton swung himself up over the wheel of the loaded wagon and lit the lantern on the dashboard.

"Don't worry about me, Leonie," he said. "This is my lucky day."

They were among the last to reach the market, and the pavings of the square were already strewn with paper and with ribbons of cabbage-leaf and carrot fern. They moved stiffly, unloading the baskets in the marketplace, and once Munday had tied the horse fast beside the other beasts, the three of them went off to a café to drink the clinging chill out of their bones.

Ayton drank at the bar with the side of his face shaded, but there were no seamen or police in the place, only the farmers and shop-keepers drinking together, with the broad "*ahs*" and "*merdes*" of their talk booming. But still he did not stay long there.

"I don't like it. I'll be off, Munday," he said.

"I'll follow along after," said Munday. "Get some sleep in the meantime, Ayton."

That was when it seemed the little man would speak, that it was hanging in his mouth, perilous, like a bell ready to ring. But he did not speak, but turned off, smiling and not quite looking at Munday and not quite looking away. The doors of the café swung wide and Munday saw him drift off amongst the people's heads and shoulders in the market-place outside.

Then Munday too went out to help get the selling over. All about were the stalls where clean, sound vegetables had been for sale; hard green heads of lettuce, white turnips, and carrots scrubbed pink and clean as wax. From hour to hour, Quespelle came out from the café and looked in sour scorn at the others who were already stacking up their empty baskets to depart. An officer of the police was beginning to promenade over the strewn ground, casting long glances at those who lingered, for the square must be neat and clean again by nine o'clock.

From hour to hour Quespelle brought his prices down, *sou* by *sou* lowering them so that the cheap dealers came back again and fingered his meager things.

"These others," said Quespelle, speaking low and scornfully to Munday as he jerked his head toward the prosperous farmers who were leaving for home with their baskets empty and money in their pockets. "They've done what's called building up a clientele. And they've got that clientele tight and fast in the hollows of their hands. They'd buy *merde* from them if they offered it! It's nothing to do with the quality of the goods. It's the secret of salesmanship, having a clientele . . . "

Then back into the café for another drink to solace him, then out again when some time had passed, his tireless voice going on in scorn. The horse had fallen asleep in the shafts, his soft loose nose nearly touching the cobbles, and the hairs on his quivering lower lip trembling with each blast of sleep he blew. But after three hours the morning was still fresh and young, and Munday set to stacking the half-emptied baskets on the cart. Quespelle bore off a measure of turnips to settle his round at the cafe. He jerked up the horse's head as he returned, and Munday in the light of day saw that he was clean for a change and prepared for heaven knew what, wearing a clean denim coat and no apron, a shirt that Leonie had boiled white for him with patches of other cloth laid carefully at the elbows, and highly polished boots. As Quespelle helped them load, he held the half-empty baskets at a distance from his good clothes, and when he had done he washed his hands and wrists carefully under the running spout at the fountain. There he stood drying his short black hands in an immaculate handkerchief, and smoothing back his mustaches.

"I'm leaving the horse tied up here for a time," he said. He buttoned his coat and winked an eye at Munday. "I'll take the money you made this morning," he said. "If I'm being forced out of the vicinity, I have a social call to make in the quarter."

CHAPTER XXX

AYTON would be in the room, waiting; asleep on the bed, maybe, but waiting. The dust might be lying on the books and the piano, and the blankets folded square as they had been when they left, and Ayton fallen asleep on top of them. There was no sense to the haste that was driving Munday through the streets, there was no need for it. Ayton would lie asleep for awhile, and when he roused they would wash their faces and go out and drink coffee in the sun together.

But when he had reached the quays, Munday scarcely dared lift his eyes to the top windows of the house at the corner, for whenever Ayton walked into a place he went first to the windows and threw them open. Or might it be, if the shutters were drawn, that he had left them closed for the sake of sleep and darkness? But the sight of the shutters thrown wide would bring the spittle to Munday's tongue again, would quiet his hands in his pockets. *The shutters wide open*, he admonished his soul, and he turned his eyes boldly up to the mansard rooms on the corner. There they were, standing wide to let in the light of day. He crossed the street running, and rapped at the *concierge's* window for letters before going up the stairs. There was only a paper from England and nothing else.

"And your key!" she called after him when he had started up the staircase.

"My key," said Munday.

Even when he had repeated this it seemed to bear no meaning to him. He turned back and the *concierge* put the key in his hand.

"Your friend left it for you," she said, "when he came for the piano."

"The piano?" asked Munday. He stood there in bewilderment. "The piano. Oh, yes."

He stood in the hallway with the English newspaper and the key of his room in his hand, waiting for the puzzle to be solved, and then he started up the stairs again, and climbed flight after flight, until he had reached the top. Then he put the key in the lock and turned it, not knowing what he expected to see. But the room was in no disorder: the dust was drifted deep on the books, and in the center the iron stove stood as it had always stood on its arched beautiful legs. From the alcove came only gaping silence, the awesome hush of void and absence. There was no paper, no hint of explanation. He looked at the four dark rings on the floor where the piano had left its footprints. There was nothing else; like the score of a symphony savagely torn across, the music had finished there.

When he had come down the shaft of the stairway to the ground again, he tapped at the *concierge's* window. He must lean low to talk to her through the sly little window in the hall.

"What time did Mr. Ayton come for the piano?" he asked.

"He came early," she said. "Before seven o'clock. With one of the young ladies."

"I see," said Munday, nodding as though he knew.

"The handsome one," said the *concierge*.

"Yes," Munday said, and he left the key with her.

"And the camion and movers with them," she added.

He walked out into the street with the paper from England still in his hand. He crossed to the other side and walked along by the inland basins, watching the lizards run before him like quick-silver in the dust. And like this were thoughts of Ayton flickering in panic through the dust of his bewilderment. The sun on the stones was warm through the worn soles of his shoes, and before him lay the desert of the city, scorching and blind and no direction offered.

He walked slowly, like a man feeling his way through sleep, with the paper from England still in his hand, carrying it in his slow meandering down the coast toward Edith's house, and down the sandy path to her door. There he wandered through the garden, pacing back and forth over the foot-prints of his own lost, seeking feet. After a while he thought that the sun itself must be fading away, for the power of it was not so violent. On the side of the house a vine rattled and coughed in the breeze, and all over the garden was a stiff, strange seaside vegetation of podded stalks and sharp gray grasses, with each blade bending down to trace its circle in the sand. The world itself seemed to have dropped away from the edge of this place and left him to survive alone upon its barren soil. On the wall of Edith's empty house tapped the vine, black and sapless, clawing at the plaster with its brittle nails. Near the gate where he had entered stood a miniature laurel tree with its branches opening and swinging like the shifting jaw of a skull. Over and over across the garden he walked, and although he wanted to think coherently of Ayton, whether to understand him or to blame him, he could not take his mind from the sight of these other things. Behind him the clouds were banking together, spreading their cold-blooded presence over the entire sky. When he turned, he could see them lying one upon the other, as sea-things might, white and boneless, obscene lovers, soft and liquescent, engulfed in embrace. The wind was beginning to blow the sand in light blasts through the garden as Munday walked from end to end of it, back and forth, back and forth, with the world shriveling about him and perishing in desolation. Even the sun had not escaped the touch of it, and he could feel it, a blind, white orb fixed on him in the cooling sky.

One minute he had been able to see the sea spreading in through the stones of the shore, and when he raised his eyes again the great dark wings of the heavens had closed over him and a shaft of light from the semaphore was striking rhythmically out from the cliff. He stood mesmerized, watching the unblinking beam cross the dark sky and the garden. He might have been deep in sleep, so numbing was the weight of bewilderment and unnamed foreboding that lay heavy on his heart.

The sea was arching and hastening in, and in the light from the semaphore the wings of lost sea birds were wildly beating. In relentless strokes came the light from the beacon swinging endlessly, endlessly at him until he could bear no more. He turned and started back through the streets of the town, and there was lamp-light in every window. In the narrow alleys mechanical pianos were playing, cats slipping between his legs, and the massive presence of the Church rebuking him. When he came to one house that had a familiar facade, he climbed its steps without effort, scarcely knowing that he climbed. It had been arranged elsewhere that he should knock on the door that inevitably appeared before him. The feet on the other side had been waiting a long time, it would seem, and now they hastened over the floor. The door opened and Mrs. Sophia stood there in the hallway's flickering light.

"What is it you want?" she cried in irritation when she saw it was only Munday.

"Have you seen Ayton?" he asked.

"Yes," said Mrs. Sophia. "He's gone off with them. They had a roll of money as thick as your fist."

She faced him, hostile and bitter, her dim eyes laced with scarlet veins.

"I've told the police," she said. "They can't get away with it. They can't take my daughter off like that. She's under age still." She looked at him, and suddenly her old mouth fell to pieces with her grief. "Listen, Mr. Munday," she said. "Maybe you yourself could do something. I want my daughter. I'm an old woman. There's nothing left to me," she said.

She stood swaying in the slice of musk and the lamp's uneasy light in the doorway.

"Listen Mr. Munday," she said, but he had gone down the steps to the street, still holding the English paper in his hand.

★ ★ ★

The rose-trees were dug out of the ground and sold, no doubt, and the wire fence had been taken down. All about were the gaping graves of the flowering plants, the shrubs, and the rose-trees. There would be no place for the geraniums anywhere they might be going: Bruneval, Etretat, Fécamp, Dieppe, northwards out of Le Havre and away from the province of Rouen.

Quespelle was opening a bottle of red wine in the shade under the ardoises and Leonie slicing a knot of bread in two, drawing the knife through toward her heart. They had set the dog free for the last day in the garden, and it ran swiftly through the grasses, following the scents of life that laced the ground. Quespelle leaned down and selected a cigarette from Munday's packet that had fallen near the doorway.

"If I had the money for a fight in court," he said, "I could get the best of them." He set down his glass and wiped his mustaches in his hand. "From the point of view of law," he said, speaking like a judge in the highest court speaking, "A man can't be put off the land like this."

Munday took up his own glass of wine and, drinking, he could see through the thick bottom of the tumbler the blue of Leonie's dress and the colors of the garden, as if through the eye of a kaleidoscope, the changes in the valley gathering and shifting and breaking. When she sat down at the table, Quespelle walked out into the sun.

"But what if you should not leave us at Dieppe after all," she was saying to Munday, seated there below him, holding her breath softly in her teeth. "There is beautiful country beyond on the coast," she said.

Now they were alone and Munday heard her voice speaking gently to him, summoning him as if to arouse him from a dream. Her words were summoning him from disaster, embracing and possessing him. Below in the valley lay the narrow canal, and the green, green marshlands. From the steamboats passing, spirals of smoke drifted upward like duck feathers on the air.

He poured out another glass of wine, in such haste that it spilled over the boards of the table.

"No, I'll go off to somewhere else," he said. "I'm done with the country for a time."

But then she began speaking again, speaking words that might have been spoken once as a child to him, but this he could not remember. He did not know whether or not his mother had ever sat so, with her hands opened out on the table, or if any woman had ever sat so, speaking, knowing only that he must come close to the gulf stream of her warm voice in the icy chaos of the storm. She was speaking to him as though life were just beginning rather than coming to an end.

"I don't know when I stopped believing him," she said. "I don't know. I don't know when it began to seem harder to have him stay here than to have him go." So went the warm current of her love, flowing, drifting through the afternoon as though there were many afternoons before them, and the stream never to run shallow. "I don't know how it began or if it ended," she was saying. "Perhaps it will never end, and when it began perhaps it was never

226

the way I thought it was. When the two of you came here, like saints coming, I've never felt the same way since, for that's the way my courage divided, half in you and half in me, and if you go too there's only a part of it left to me. Even the day you fought with Quespelle I was through with fainting or crying or dying even, how it happened or why it was this way I don't know."

The river of her voice wound smooth and unbroken under the beams, flowing deeper and deeper into the shade, lapping gently, gently at the rafters, drifting, submerging him, like the waters of willing death. But abruptly he roused and said:

"There's yours and Quespelle's child on the way. Whatever happens next has nothing to do with me."

"Ah, no!" Leonie cried. "You don't believe that, do you? You must have known. Now that Ayton's gone I can speak of it openly. But you must have known," she said. "It isn't Quespelle's child."

Munday set his glass down on the table.

"But whose?" he asked. For a moment no glimmer of light was cast on his bewildered incomprehension. "But whose child then?" he repeated. And in some part of his brain Ayton's voice began the elaborate explanation, the "oi" and the "ing" of the Cockney accent imploring for understanding. "Whose child?" Munday asked again, and now the light was as blinding as a midsummer day, and when Leonie began to speak he cried out, "No, no, don't say it!" But after a moment or two he was able to speak gently and quietly to her, saying, "We are the two survivors of a ship that foundered and together we must make the long swim back to shore."

EDITOR'S NOTE

KAY BOYLE *long felt an urgent need to rewrite this early novel (1931) and give it a "second life." In August 1990, after two years of revision and clarifying the themes she felt were obscured by her youthful tendencies to overwrite, she read the final typescript and gave it her blessing.*